The Stolen Bride

Olivia West

The Stolen Bride

Published by Olivia West

Copyright © 2019 by Olivia West

ISBN 978-1-07203-744-6

First printing, 2019

www.OliviaWestBooks.com

Table of Contents

Chapter 1

Her every dream was coming true. Her perfect plans were falling into place the way she'd always pictured that they would, and she couldn't imagine that there was a luckier girl in the entire world. Life was unfolding just the way she had always wanted. She had it all. The fabulous career *and* the wonderful fiancé. From the depths of her soul to the tips of her toes, she was completely thrilled. Her life felt like a modern-day fairy tale complete with all of the lovely and ultra-chic trimmings. However, Lindsey Thomas was not a frivolous fool. Not by any stretch of the imagination. She'd worked hard to get to where she was—attending a great school, interning for several designers, working her way up the corporate ladder, all the while managing to find and date the most amazing guy in her valuable free time. She'd known all along that her dreams wouldn't simply materialize without the proper foresight and planning. Therefore, the moment Patrick Crawford had slid the hefty three-carat engagement ring on her finger a little less than two months ago, she had immediately shifted some of her laser-sharp focus onto starting work on every wedding detail imaginable. She ate, drank and slept wedding details. Even between hectic meetings at work, she perused through invitation samples and font options.

Just in the last week, Lindsey and Patrick had toured several potential wedding venues, and had spent plenty of time at each of them, trying to picture how the space would work for an early spring wedding. It wasn't all that easy to envision when they were experiencing the record-breaking, hot, humid July weather that was currently descending upon New York in earnest. Lindsey already yearned for the crisp, cool weather they could expect for their April ceremony. She was so over the incessant heat and the number it was working on her normally perfect and bouncy reddish-brown curls.

Thankfully, tonight the weather wasn't quite as miserable as it had been as of late, Lindsey mused from her stance on the stone terrace. She took in the elegant party taking place all around her at the immaculate Greenwich mansion of her wealthy, soon-to-be in-laws. After taking a sip of cold, crisp champagne from the crystal flute in her hand, she tossed her hair over her shoulder, ready to make another round through the large crowd that had gathered in her and Patrick's honor. Although the Crawfords' mansion was an hour away from the city, where she and most of her friends and family lived, the posh atmosphere was well worth the scenic drive to Connecticut.

When Patrick's parents had offered to host their engagement party, Lindsey had happily accepted. She loved Patrick's parents, they loved her, and this was the perfect opportunity for the two families to mingle. It had been a true pleasure helping Patrick's mother plan the elegant soiree, as they shared similar tastes and a penchant for party planning.

"Having fun, sweetheart?" Patrick asked, coming up behind her and placing his arm leisurely around her waist.

"Yes! It's such a wonderful party," she replied turning and smiling brightly up at him, "and I think everyone is really having a great time. It's getting me excited about our wedding."

Patrick didn't say anything, just tugged nervously at his pale pink necktie that perfectly matched the shade of Lindsey's strapless, designer dress. She'd insisted that they match.

"Everything okay?" Lindsey asked, noting Patrick's worried expression.

"Yeah, yeah. Everything's fine. Just ... wow, you know? It finally feels real—we're going to get married," Patrick said, his eyes wide, his skin clammy.

"Yep, and there isn't a happier girl in the whole wide world than this one right here," Lindsey said, leaning in close and putting her head on Patrick's shoulder reassuringly.

"You're such a sweetheart, Lindsey," Patrick replied nonchalantly, preoccupied as he scanned the room and sipped from his tumbler full of the finest whiskey.

She couldn't put her finger on it, but something was wrong with Patrick. However, as friends and family buzzed around them with excited energy, Lindsey put the notion aside, but not before making a mental note to ask him if everything was okay later. She certainly wasn't going to press him for information with so much going on around them right now. Too many people needed their attention right now.

"Lindseyyyy!"

Hearing her name disrupted the potentially worrisome turn of her thoughts. Kate Welling, Lindsey's best friend since they'd roomed together their freshman year at NYU, had arrived and was making her way across the huge room toward her. Lindsey hurried over in her six-inch heels to greet her bubbly friend.

"Kate, you're late," Lindsey teased, giving her petite friend a warm hug.

"Did you expect me to actually make it on time? In the past seven years of friendship, have I ever managed to be on time anywhere?" Kate asked her, only half kidding. She had a point, Lindsey thought. Punctuality had never been, and probably would never be, her best friend's strong suit.

"Okay, okay. It's just the engagement party. But as the maid of honor, you have to arrive to everything else on time," Lindsey reminded her.

"Just lie to me about the start time—build me in a thirty-minute cushion," Kate suggested, taking a glass of champagne garnished with strawberries from a passing waiter's tray. Lindsey rolled her eyes at her ridiculous but wonderful friend. She and Kate were the exact opposite in so many ways. As a clothing buyer and trend spotter working for Lord & Taylor, Lindsey thrived on details, plans, and organization, while Kate, an up-and-coming fashion designer, focused strictly on her passion, never paying attention to schedules, plans or anything else that remotely resembled organization or tidy order. Lindsey truly felt sorry for Kate's assistant, Olivia, knowing her hands stayed full keeping Kate in line and where she needed to be.

Hooking her arm through Kate's, Lindsey noted the wildly patterned gown she wore, something only Kate could pull off, especially at a subdued engagement party. Lindsey led them over to where Patrick stood chatting with some of his colleagues from his firm. She smiled with pride as she watched her fiancé in his element. Patrick was always so confident in his work as a brilliant attorney. A partnership at his firm would certainly be in his future.

"Hello there, Patrick. Nice to see you, again," Kate said. She gave Patrick a quick, somewhat awkward hug and a pasted-on smile.

"Likewise, Kate. I was speaking with your parents just a few minutes ago," Patrick said, making stiff, but polite conversation. For being the two most important people in Lindsey's life, they surprisingly had very little in common and could barely tolerate one another for longer than five minutes, much to her chagrin.

"Oh, I haven't seen them yet. I think I'll go find them," she said, swiftly excusing herself to go hunt down Mr. and Mrs. Welling among the crowd. Lindsey linked her arm back through Patrick's and pretended to be interested as he talked shop with his work friends, but she couldn't help feeling slightly envious as she watched the flounce of Kate's floral fuchsia gown disappear through the crowded room. Kate was such a free spirit.

As the party began winding down a couple of hours later, Lindsey let out a breath she hadn't even realized she'd been holding. Her cheeks ached from constantly smiling, and as Patrick stood by her side, bidding goodbye to a group of family members heading toward the door, Lindsey stretched her back as inconspicuously as possible. The decision to wear sky-high heels didn't seem all that smart in retrospect, no matter how killer her legs may have looked in them.

"Darlings, I think the party was a success, and Jim and I literally could not be any happier for the two of you," Patrick's mother said sweetly after the last few party stragglers were politely escorted to the door.

"Thanks, Mrs. Crawford. It means so much to us that you and Mr. Crawford hosted such a beautiful party in our honor. My parents are thrilled to be having you and Mr. Crawford over for dinner next week, also," Lindsey said to her elegant future mother-in-law, leaning in to give her a light kiss on the cheek. Mrs. Crawford gave off the gentle scent of soft powder and peonies—a scent that managed to be understated, feminine and distinctly wealthy.

"We are delighted to visit with your parents anytime, Lindsey. They are such lovely people," Mrs. Crawford replied, "Now, if you two can handle the last few details with the staff, Jim and I are going to retire for the night. I'm quite exhausted after so much fun!"

Lindsey assured them that she and Patrick could handle seeing the caterer and his staff on their way and oversee the locking up of the house. Besides, Jensen, the Crawfords' butler, would go behind them and make sure no detail was left unchecked. Mr. and Mrs. Crawford certainly had no reason to worry.

"Hey, can I talk to you for a minute?" Patrick asked after his parents had headed upstairs to their private wing.

"Sure, honey. Of course," she replied. He took Lindsey by the hand as she was still nodding her agreement and led her out onto the terrace. For a moment, Lindsey thought he possibly wanted to wax poetical and maybe dance with her in the moonlight—something he had done on occasion when they were in college—but the look in his eyes told her something much heavier than dancing was currently on his mind.

"What's wrong, Patrick?" she asked, a strange, foreboding weight settling deep within the pit of her stomach.

"Lindsey, you know that I love you. I really do. More than anything. You're an amazing, beautiful, smart woman and I know that I'm damn lucky to have you," he took a deep breath before continuing, nervously pacing across the terrace, unable to meet Lindsey's eyes, "but despite knowing how lucky I am and how amazing you are, I can't do this, Lindsey. I just can't."

"You can't do what?" Lindsey asked quietly after a beat, her voice still and calm despite the crazed turmoil roiling within her as his words registered.

"This," he gestured between the two of them. "I thought I was ready for the ring, the commitment, and the whole nine yards, but tonight, everything grew far too real for me. I'm not ready to get married, Lindsey."

"Is there someone else?" Lindsey asked the dreaded question, afraid of the answer.

"No! I just said that I love you—I wouldn't ever do that to you," Patrick said, his eyes downcast.

"So … you love me, you just don't love me enough to marry me?" Lindsey said, too shocked to cry or make any other type of scene as she stared at the man who was shattering her dreams.

"That's not what I meant. I mean, come on, doesn't it feel like we're just doing this because it seems to be time to take the next step? It scares me, Lindsey. Especially the way you have everything detailed out on a timeline up until the very day of our wedding."

"It's good to be organized," she defended, her voice cracking with emotion.

"But where's the spark? The excitement of spontaneity? Having everything planned out is just seriously freaking me out right now, and I have to take a step back and reevaluate what I want from life."

"I'm so sorry, Patrick. Sorry that I have a brain and a plan, but mostly that I loved you enough to include you in that plan," Lindsey spat out. "We're through!" she shouted behind her, her initial shock turning to anger as she turned on her heels and marched back inside. She grabbed her purse and left the mansion without even taking one glance back at Patrick.

***

"Okay, Lindsey. Enough is enough. I know this whole situation totally sucks, but you have to leave this apartment. You've been cooped up in here since the party!" Kate said, standing at the foot of Lindsey's bed with her hands on her hips.

"God, Kate. It's only been three days, and my fiancé, who happened to be my boyfriend for five years before he became my fiancé, just ended our engagement out of the blue. At our engagement party no less. It's kind of big damn deal and excuse me if I'm just a little upset," Lindsey said, eyeing the diamond that still sparkled on her finger. She hadn't mustered the nerve to take it off just yet. It made the whole breakup too real if she took off the ring. The anger she'd initially felt when she'd left Patrick on the terrace had turned the tide to a deep sadness the moment that she'd pulled out of the Crawfords' private drive and headed back to her apartment in New York. It didn't help that Patrick hadn't even called to check on her in the past three days either.

"Lindsey, have you eaten anything?" Kate said, peering warily at Lindsey, propped against a mountain of colorful pillows with her hair in a messy bun, still wearing her rattiest old pajamas with streaks of mascara and makeup smudges beneath her puffy eyes. "Or showered?"

"No and no. But I sure have found the time to drink," Lindsey muttered sarcastically, waving an empty wine bottle she'd pulled from beneath the covers at Kate.

"That's it. I'm taking matters into my own hands," Kate said, flipping the gray coverlet off Lindsey. Lindsey recoiled, curling up her knees in protest.

"What the hell, Kate? Let me grieve," Lindsey moaned, flopping back onto the mattress and covering her face with a throw pillow to block the light as Kate whipped the striped curtains back, letting in the midmorning sunshine and revealing the pretty New York City sights outlined by the most vibrant of blue skies.

"No more of this, Lindsey, I gave you three days, but you are starting to creep into self-destruction mode, which you must know as your best friend, I simply can't let that happen. You've got to get up, get going, take a shower, eat something and get back to work."

"I took the whole week off," Lindsey said, turning onto her stomach when Kate took her pillow shield away.

"He's not worth this, Lindsey! I never thought he deserved you anyway, but I kept my mouth shut because you seemed happy. Or at least happy enough. But seriously, Lindsey, you deserve a man, not a dweeby little trust fund douchebag."

"You have your own trust fund if I'm not mistaken," Lindsey's muffled voice pointed out.

"Yeah, but I don't touch it and I don't brag about it, that's for sure. I swear, Patrick's trust fund was his favorite thing to talk about with anyone," Kate said, sticking her finger down her throat and making a gagging sound.

"Well, for whatever flaws he may have had, he was intelligent, kind and thoughtful, not to mention handsome," Lindsey said, tearing up as she glanced at the picture of the two of them on her mirrored nightstand.

"If you like that way-too-skinny, hipster-looking kind of guy." Kate rolled her eyes. "So are you guys broken up, or taking a step back or what?"

"In my mind, it's over. How can we go back? He clearly doesn't want to marry me, so what? Am I supposed to be just a permanent girlfriend for the rest of forever? It was time to take the next step in our relationship. If he doesn't want to take the next step, then we aren't moving forward," Lindsey said, starting to sob now. Kate sighed, and flopped onto the bed with her, taking Lindsey into her arms and smoothing her hair away from her face.

"I know this sucks, Lindsey. There's no other word to describe it. I'm so sorry you're having to go through this," Kate comforted. "Maybe he just needs some time?"

"I can't risk my heart with him anymore," she cried. "He took it out and stomped all over it!"

"Have you told anyone else the news yet?"

"No, it's just too awful. Not only is my heart completely broken, but having to face everybody and tell them what happened and relive the terrible scene over and over again in my mind? I can't even imagine! This sucks!" Lindsey cried, a fresh spate of tears rolling down her reddened cheeks.

"What can I do to help you? Please, tell me something that I can do to make this better."

"There's nothing you can do, unless you have a hole I can go crawl in and hide inside. I don't want to face the world just yet."

A lightbulb clicked on for Kate. "I may not have a hole, but I have something even better—my family's beach house in the Hamptons."

"Kate, I don't feel like being around people and going on vacation right now. I can't pretend to be happy. I just can't."

"No, there's no one there right now. The whole family is planning on heading up there next week, but right now, it's totally empty. Why don't you head up there and spend a few days by yourself and let the sun and surf heal your soul? Nothing beats the beach when it comes to making you feel better—you and I both know that to be true. We've sworn by that very motto for years, so there's no way you can deny it."

"Are you sure your parents wouldn't mind?" Lindsey asked, the idea of getting away starting to appeal to her just the tiniest bit. At least it was something.

"Of course not! You are practically family—you know that they love you like their own daughter!"

"Have you told them about Patrick and me?"

"No, I haven't said anything to anyone yet."

"Okay, good. I'm not ready for everyone's pity. I'm still really busy pitying myself."

"So you'll go? Please tell me you'll go, and you'll sit in the sun, and read and eat tons of chocolate and watch romantic comedies and drink lots of wine."

"I'll go, but I can only promise the drinking part—I'm not so sure about the rest."

"Check in with me regularly, though, okay? I don't want you passing out on the beach and getting third-degree sunburns due to sorrowful drunkenness."

"I promise—I won't do anything stupid that would involve public drunkenness or third-degree burns. I just need to hide from the world for a minute."

"I wish I could go with you, but my couture show is this week and I can't leave the city until it's pulled off without a hitch. I'm going up next week with the family if you decide to stay a little longer," Kate told her.

"I really want to be alone anyway," she replied honestly.

Within a couple of hours, and with a lot of help from Kate, Lindsey was showered, dressed and packed for her impromptu trip to the Hamptons. In a bright pink racerback tank, white shorts and a straw sunhat covering most of her reddish-brown curls, hiding behind her oversized sunglasses, Lindsey looked much more chipper than she actually felt.

After finishing a bowl of granola and yogurt at Kate's insistence, Lindsey settled into the back of the Welling family's private car for the trip to the coast. Kate had called for the car, not wanting Lindsey to take the jitney bus to the coast in her fragile state.

"Thanks, Kate—I may be semi-hating you right now, but I know, at some point, I'll look back and be happy that you made me put one foot in front of another even though I don't want to do anything but lie in my bed, drink wine, and wallow in my sadness,"

Lindsey said, peering up at her from the backseat window with her dark shades in place. She couldn't even attempt to pretend to smile at that moment.

"No problem. Now, go forth and lie around, drink wine and wallow in the beautiful sun by the ocean," Kate said with a wink, waving her off. "And try to find a man while you're there—hot rebound sex would really do you a world of good!" Kate called out in jest as the car pulled away from the curb. She smiled sheepishly as two elderly women power-walked by at the exact moment the brazen words left her lips.

Lindsey slipped her headphones on and slumped in the seat, sighing sadly, glad that she no longer had to pretend that she had it somewhat together. Kate meant well, but she had no idea how Lindsey really felt. When Patrick had called off their engagement, Lindsey's world had been turned upside down and she was still puzzled as to how she was going to start putting it back together again. The whole process overwhelmed her past the point of comprehension.

Normally, she was on top of things. She had it together, she never lost her cool, she planned everything down to the last tiny detail. But now, now she could hardly muster enough interest to get herself properly dressed for the day, much less try and figure out what to do now that her entire life plan was shattered into millions of pieces.

Maybe the trip to the Hamptons would help. She really didn't care about vacationing all that much at the moment, but at least, she wouldn't have to deal with the situation for a few days. She could put off the inevitable just a little while longer. Her stomach sank every time she pictured having to tell someone that she was no longer engaged—that all her plans were going down the drain. She wasn't ready to face all of that yet. With so much whirling around inside of her mind, Lindsey closed her eyes, hoping she could sleep during the ride out to the coast. At least when she was asleep, she wasn't thinking about all that she had to face. Sleep also afforded her a temporary reprieve from the raw aching of her wounded heart.

Chapter 2

"Thanks so much for your help with my bags," Lindsey said, waving as the driver nodded and told her goodbye. She closed the front door and looked around the foyer, once again floored at the Welling family's wealth. Just the foyer of the enormous East Hampton mansion elegantly showcased luxury with the set of Art Deco crystal chandeliers hanging from the arched ceiling, the plush Oriental rug and the intricately wainscoted walls. Natural light streamed in from the bank of windows flanking either side of the broad, glass-paned double doors, and everything was decorated in shades of white, steel gray or ocean blue.

The Welling family's driver had taken her bags to the master suite on the second floor, so she went upstairs right away, trying to remember from her past visits to the beach house exactly where the master suite was located. She turned left at the top of the stairs and made her way down a lengthy hallway, past dozens of doors and a couple of small sitting areas to a set of polished French doors at the end of the hall.

Once inside, she continued to gaze around in awe, her spirits lifting considerably. How could anyone be all that depressed surrounded by such luxury? The master suite was bigger than Lindsey's entire Chelsea apartment. The room flowed with the same soft beachy tones as the rest of the mansion, and bleached linen panels framed the window alcove that looked out onto the sparkling Atlantic Ocean. Through an open arched doorway, the master bathroom housed the biggest spa tub she'd ever seen, and of course, it was positioned where you could open the shuttered windows and listen to the sounds of the ocean while relaxing in the tub.

Trailing her fingertips along the Egyptian cotton coverlet, reveling in the soft, expensive feel, Lindsey sort of wanted to smile for the first time since Patrick called off their engagement. She had the run of this luxurious mansion for the next several days. She could walk around naked and eat ice cream in the king-size bed if she chose to do so.

With a burst of energy and a sudden urge to immediately hit the beach, she hurried to change into her classic black bikini. Pulling her hair up in a loose bun, she slid on her aviator sunglasses and padded down to the kitchen barefooted. She didn't bother to look for a proper glass, but instead opened a bottle of white wine and took the whole thing out with her to sit by the pool that sat mere yards from the sandy beach. The pool was the best of both worlds. She could enjoy the sights of the beach without having to get sandy.

Lying on a blue lounge chair beneath the shade of an umbrella, sunning her legs and listening to the crash of the waves as she sipped from the bottle was just what the doctor had ordered. She could definitely get used to this. It was even possible to block out the horrid fact that she wasn't engaged to be married anymore. She was beginning to firmly believe, now more than ever, that the beach was a medicinal remedy that could cure just about anything that plagued the soul.

Later that evening, she ordered in takeout from a local Italian restaurant. After eating her dinner standing at the kitchen counter, she strolled along the beach as the sun started to set. It wasn't until she'd tucked herself into the crisp sheets that the sad ache returned to her heart and the tears began to flow again.

Even at the beach, surrounded by the beauty of nature and the luxury of the Wellings' home, the pain she'd been trying to avoid had finally caught up with her—it had just waited to creep up on her when the house was quiet and the silver moonlight streamed through the windows, just like the other night on the terrace when Patrick single-handedly crumbled her dreams with just a handful of life-altering words.

***

Morning came as it always did. The sun relentlessly rose in the east and shined directly into her eyes from the open bay windows. As she squinted against the brightness, Lindsey made a mental note to make sure to pull the curtains closed each night before going to bed for the rest of the week. Glancing at the clock on the bedside table, she groaned to see that it wasn't even seven o'clock yet. Resolved to her fate, knowing there was no way she would be able to get back to sleep in her unfamiliar surroundings, Lindsey hopped up and quickly dressed in running shorts and a hot pink sports bra.

After running a few miles along the shoreline, she headed back in. She ate a granola bar while standing by the kitchen counter before showering off and changing back into her swimsuit. She planned on practically living in a swimsuit this week. A swimsuit and her comfy pajamas. That was all she needed.

While it was still morning, Lindsey made her way down to the beach with a book and planted herself there for the next several hours, alternately lying in the sun and wading in the shallow waves. The beach wasn't very crowded along this particular stretch of the coast—it was mostly privately owned, so only a few dozen people were scattered along the shoreline as far as she could see in either direction.

What was she going to do? she thought as she watched a couple and their toddler splash in the waves. Marrying Patrick had been an integral part of her life plan. She had the successful career, the fun city life, but she was ready for a family, a home. Now, it felt like she had to basically start over from scratch. She'd spent over five years with Patrick. Five years of her life wasted!

She didn't want to even think about dating someone else. The idea was not even the least bit appealing. She'd always loathed the entire process of dating. Why couldn't you just find someone, decide you were good together and that be the end of it? None of this "I'm not ready" horseshit. She shook her head furiously, getting so pissed once again at the thought of what Patrick had done to her. It wasn't so much just that she was just dying to get married, but more so that she wanted to be settled, have that we're-together-and-that's-the-end-of-it commitment that she had thought that she had with him. They'd had a great five years, what the hell was wrong with getting married and making everything official?

A knot formed in her stomach as an unsettling thought popped unbidden into her mind. What if he'd just gotten tired of her? What if he couldn't imagine spending his life with her because he didn't find her all that interesting? He had complained about her lack of spontaneity after all.

She snapped closed the novel she'd hadn't even looked at in the past ten minutes. While at the beach, she resolved to try and be more spontaneous. Maybe she would take up a new water sport or get a tattoo. Do something that no one expected.

Around lunchtime, she figured it was time to head into town and get a few fresh groceries, not really wanting to survive on packaged granola bars, wine and unhealthy takeout food for the duration of her trip. Lindsey packed up her book, bottle of water and towel, tossing everything into her beach bag except for the earbuds and iPhone to which she was currently listening. She retraced her earlier steps back up to the planked walkway across the dunes that became a pebbled trail before reaching the pool and patio area at the back of the traditional Hamptons mansion.

As she stepped through the French doors, the rush of the cool air inside the house felt glorious against her heated skin. The walk back to the house with the scorching midday sun beating down on her had left her hot and sweaty and way past ready for a shower. She headed straight up the stairs, pulling her hair out of its messy bun, and untying the back of her bikini as she walked down the never-ending hall. Just as she reached her room, she tossed the bag by the door, pulled out her earphones and placed them within the bag. She slipped out of her sandals, and was about to finish pulling off her top when a noise somewhere down the hall stopped her in her tracks.

Terrified, Lindsey slowly turned around in the doorway of the suite to see a man standing at the top of the stairs staring at her, his eyes wide in surprise. Her jaw dropped in surprise as she scrambled to make sure that her untied top was still covering all of the necessary parts.

"Lindsey?" he asked, averting his eyes politely as Lindsey righted her barely there wardrobe. She breathed a sigh of relief when she recognized the visitor.

"Harris, what are you doing here?" Lindsey asked Kate's older brother. He was five years older than Kate and a renowned author who lived in upstate Maine. She'd only been around him a handful of times since meeting Kate their freshman year of college seven years ago.

"My parents and Kate are headed here next week. I came early to finish editing my latest book. I didn't know that anyone was going to be here ..." he trailed off. While he spoke, Lindsey had grabbed the swimsuit cover-up she'd tossed into her beach bag earlier and thrown it over her scantily clad body.

"Just let me pack up my stuff, and I can be out of your way and back to the city as soon as I've showered. Kate thought that no one would be here," Lindsey said, explaining her presence in his family's mansion.

"You don't have to pack up. Why don't you go ahead and shower and dress, and then we can talk in the kitchen once you're finished?" he suggested, his bags still on his arms.

"Okay, I won't be but a few minutes," Lindsey replied, darting inside the suite and shutting the door behind her, leaving Harris still standing at the top of the stairs. She gulped in air, trying to calm her pounding heart. This had to be the most embarrassing thing that had ever happened to her! He probably thought she was squatting in his family's beach house or something equally horrifying. And here she was in the master suite—she should have taken one of the smaller guest rooms down the hall. What had she been thinking?

Lindsey rapidly undressed and headed to the enormous standing shower. After she'd rinsed off, she quickly dried her hair and threw on a cheerful, floral sundress, foregoing all makeup except a little mascara, before hurrying back downstairs to find Harris. She only realized once she'd turned the corner and found herself in the huge kitchen with its whitewashed fireplace, marble countertops and keeping room, that she was still barefoot.

She'd gotten used to padding around the house sans shoes, but it didn't boost her confidence as she saw Harris pulling out a couple of matching mugs from a cabinet. He was wearing a crisp white shirt, well-fitted jeans and tortoiseshell glasses—he looked every bit the part of the perfect intellectual scholar/GQ model hybrid. Despite the slight bit of intimidation at the sight of Kate's handsome older brother, Lindsey perked up at the smell of coffee brewing.

She took the opportunity to study him before he noticed her. For Lindsey, it was easy to see now why so many articles about Harris made sure to mention how handsome he was. Harris was tall, dark-haired and broad-shouldered. He also had the same olive complexion and hazel eyes as Kate and Mrs. Welling, supposedly inherited from their Greek roots.

"Hello, Harris," she finally said when she mustered up the nerve to greet him. This whole unexpected situation had her out of her natural element. She wasn't used to feeling flustered and nervous—she typically thrived with her ability to remain calm and collected at all times. But coming off the heels of her recent engagement debacle, she really wasn't feeling like her normal, confident, level-headed self. It also didn't help that she felt like she was trespassing in his family's home.

"Hey there. Coffee?" He smiled in an easy greeting as he gestured to the plain white cups he'd placed on the marble countertop. She nodded and took a seat at the kitchen island while he searched for the sugar and cream.

"There isn't much in the pantry or fridge, other than packaged staples," Lindsey explained. Harris stepped into the walk-in pantry and came back a few seconds later with a container holding packets of sugar and half-and-half.

"This is my secret stash. I randomly pop down here unannounced, but the cleaning crew regularly throws out anything they think will spoil. These little packets are good to have on hand. I'll have to mention to Mom that she needs to add these to the staple list," he told her. Harris set the sugar and cream packets on the island in front of Lindsey and pulled a couple of spoons from one of the drawers, too.

After he'd poured them both a steaming cupful of coffee, he took a seat at the island across from Lindsey. They made their coffee, each taking a sip before either said anything.

"I'm sure you're wondering what I'm doing here," Lindsey finally started, ready to get the uncomfortable conversation over with sooner rather than later.

"And you're probably wondering the same thing about me."

"No, not at all. This is your family's home—you can come and go as you please. Sure, I was surprised to see you, but you have every right to be here."

"That doesn't change the fact that you didn't expect me to show up here. I came down a few days early to write, like I told you. The beach, the solitude—it's the perfect place for me to get a good bit of work done in peace with a fresh change of scenery. So, what brings you here?" he asked, picking up his coffee and taking another sip, his eyes studying Lindsey intently.

Lindsey held the warm mug with both hands, suddenly feeling cold despite the bright sunshine outside. "Kate thought it would be a good idea for me to get away for a few days," she said, having a hard time meeting Harris' eyes.

"Is she coming up, too?"

"No, she couldn't get away because of her show, and she figured that I probably needed to be alone anyway."

"Do you mind me asking if everything is alright?"

Lindsey really looked at him then, and she figured the look on her face must have answered his question far better than any words would have.

"Don't worry—you don't have to tell me. It's none of my business anyway."

"Look," Lindsey stood up, "I'm really sorry for this mix-up. You thought the home was unoccupied and I hadn't expected—based on Kate's insistence—that anyone would be here either. I'll just pack up my things and take the next bus back to the city. It really isn't a problem." She started to head out of the kitchen.

"Wait, Lindsey. Hear me out. Obviously, my sister offered you the use of the beach house, and I'm sure it was with good reason. It's a huge house. Please don't leave—I'll go. I seriously don't mind."

Lindsey shook her head furiously. "No way, this is your house, not mine. I'm not about to kick you out so that I can stay. There's no way that I could ever let you do that and not feel ridiculously guilty."

"What if we both stayed? We can keep to ourselves—the house is pretty huge—and that way you can have your alone time and I can get my editing done in the study. If you left, I would never hear the end of it from Kate, and I honestly see no problem with it anyway," he replied, sipping the last of his coffee.

She turned around and sat back down while she considered his suggestion, studying Harris to see if he really meant what he said. She wasn't totally sure how she felt about the proposal, but the house was enormous, and it really wouldn't be all that hard to keep their distance from each other.

"Are you sure?" she asked cautiously.

"I'm positive. It's seriously fine with me. It might be nice to have a little company from time to time, too—if you're up for it. Nothing crazy—maybe dinners together or something like that?"

"That would be fine with me. Actually, it would be nice to get to know you a little better, Harris. After all, your sister is my best friend, but I hardly know anything about you."

"You two have been friends since college, haven't you?"

"Ever since we roomed together freshman year," Lindsey said with a small smile.

Harris took a sip of his coffee. "Well, I know this might not mean much coming from someone that barely knows you, but I do know Kate. And I just want you to know how glad I am that she has you. You've been an amazing friend to her," he told her.

"Thanks, Harris. That really does mean a lot." She scooted off the barstool where she'd been perching during most of their chat and took her coffee mug to the sink. "I'll leave you to get settled in—I was heading into town to grab a few groceries anyway. Is there anything I can pick up for you?"

"If you don't mind, some frosted flakes and milk would be great. I could live off those for days," he joked.

Lindsey rolled her eyes and laughed. "Man can't live off cereal alone," she teased, "but I'll gladly grab a box or two for you."

He smiled at her, his eyes crinkling. "Thank you, Lindsey."

She waved behind her as she scooted out the garage door, "I'm off! See you later!" she called out cheerfully.

Chapter 3

Back from grabbing groceries, Lindsey dumped the bags on the granite countertop and swiftly set to work loading the refrigerator and putting away the staples in the pantry. She looked longingly through the kitchen's French doors that opened to the pool area. That comfy lounge chair by the pool was calling her name already.

She marinated a couple of steaks in olive oil and fresh garlic before running upstairs to change back into a swimsuit. Glancing around, she wondered where Harris had situated himself for the afternoon, but shrugged the thought away. Probably in the study, she figured. She reminded herself that he was there to do his own thing, as was she. It didn't matter what he was up to this afternoon.

She dug through her bag and found a mint-green, ruffled bikini that she had yet to wear. Quickly changing, she slid her feet into her leather flip-flops and made her way outside as fast as possible. The sun was still pretty high overhead as she settled into her favorite chair—the one that gave the best views of the beach and provided the best spot for tanning, too. Lindsey lay down on her stomach, her face pressed against her pink-and-white striped beach towel. All too soon, sweat trickled down her nose as she roasted.

When she couldn't take the heat one second longer, she hopped up and dove into the pool. As she plunged into the deep end, the cool water surrounding her was both refreshing and invigorating. She swam a couple of laps, then rested her elbows on the scalloped, stone edge and let her legs float lazily with her eyes closed.

"Mind if I join you?"

Her eyes shot open as Harris' voice startled her. Looking up, she saw him towering over her in his navy swim trunks and sunglasses, a plain white towel tossed over his muscled shoulder.

"Not at all, the water's great," she enthusiastically replied. He sat on the edge near to where she floated and eased slowly into the pool. Lindsey watched him, noting that he may have stayed busy writing, but he certainly still made time for the gym. His chest and arms were well-defined, not overly so, but just the right, appealing amount.

"I settled into the downstairs office, which faces the beach and pool, thinking the surf and sun would inspire me. Instead, I see you sunning and then jumping into the pool having a blast, and I couldn't take it any longer. I was too jealous. I had to join in on the fun."

She laughed. "The beach and pool here are absolutely fabulous. If I was cooped up inside working, I would have been jealous of me, too."

"Yeah, so I decided to do something about it." He glided under the water, swimming around a bit before coming up for air, smoothing his hair back, and looking far too much like a Greek god or a modern-day Adonis as he did so.

"So, how's old what's-his-name?" Harris asked nonchalantly as he floated around her.

Lindsey froze. "Are you asking about Patrick?"

"Yeah, you guys are engaged, aren't you?" Harris asked innocently.

"We … broke up," Lindsey admitted for the first time to anyone other than Kate.

Harris' face fell. "Oh, Lindsey. I'm so sorry. I didn't mean to pry—I really had no idea. I'm surprised Kate didn't tell me when I spoke to her earlier."

"I made her swear not to tell anyone."

"Well, I'm glad you told me. It ups this week's fun factor, don't you think?" He winked.

Lindsey stared wide-eyed at him.

"Oh no! Sorry, again. I didn't mean that the way it came out. All I meant was that we could maybe go out, hit the bars or something—with no worries of jealous significant others," he explained.

"Okay, because I was like seriously—that probably wouldn't be a good idea, the two of us," she gestured between them. "You're my best friend's brother, and I was engaged up until a week ago. My mind can't even fathom dating anyone right now."

"Yeah, yeah, of course. Totally agree," he said casually, nodding as water dripped from his hair.

"But, I am glad you're here," she admitted, "and I think we're going to be great friends and I can't wait to 'hit the bars' with you," she winked.

"It sounds really corny now that I'm hearing it repeated back to me. I think I need to get out more," he laughed.

"I'm serious though—maybe I need a night out to just let loose and have some fun. Are you really up for it?"

"Tonight?"

"Yes, tonight."

"I don't see why not," he shrugged.

"Good. We can head to the Talkhouse Bar later. Oh, and I picked up some steaks for dinner. I marinated them just like Gina does—it's my favorite marinade and I figured you would like them that way, too." Lindsey hopped out of the pool and grabbed her towel.

"Who doesn't love Mom's steaks? They're the best." Harris followed Lindsey out of the pool. "I'll get the grill going before I hit the shower," he offered.

"Thanks, that'll be great." She tossed the words over her shoulder as she headed back inside the double doors.

As she showered and blow-dried her hair, she couldn't help thinking about the crazy turn of events that had paired her with Harris for the week. She'd originally hoped to be alone so that she could fully wallow in her sorrows while scoring a killer tan and binging on wine and cherry chocolate ice cream, but hanging out with Harris, "hitting the bars," and socializing a bit now and then seemed much more interesting.

Lindsey pulled on a coral romper and threw her hair up in hot rollers before doing her makeup. It felt nice to enjoy getting ready again. Maybe there was a light at the end of the breakup tunnel she'd been forcefully dwelling in all week.

Once she'd finished getting ready, she made her way down to the kitchen to find that Harris was already working on dinner.

"I told you I would handle dinner," she said as she pulled a container of lettuce out of the refrigerator.

"But I was already showered and dressed, and I really don't mind helping," he said as he chopped tomatoes.

"Is the grill ready?"

"Yep," he nodded. "I set the steaks out, over there," he gestured with his elbow to the Pyrex dish on the countertop closest to the doors that led out to the grill.

"Well, let's get those babies going and I'll pour us a glass of pre-dinner wine," she told him, pulling a bottle of her favorite red from the pantry.

"Sounds like a plan," he said wiping his hands on a towel, finished with chopping the vegetables she'd purchased for a summer salad. He rinsed his hands before grabbing the steaks and headed outside. Lindsey followed, precariously balancing two rather full glasses of red wine in her hands.

"Whoa, that's not a glass, that's half a bottle," Harris remarked as Lindsey handed him his hefty glass. Lindsey shrugged.

"It's what Kate and I like to refer to as a 'house' glass," she explained with a smirk.

"As opposed to a standard, restaurant serving, I'm assuming?"

"Exactly." She took a sip of the pinot noir.

"Cheers, Lindsey, to a night of new friendship and fun," he said, raising his glass toward her.

"Oh, yes, cheers," she said belatedly after she'd swallowed her first sip.

Once they'd finished cooking, they sat at the table on the patio to have a nice dinner al fresco.

"Gosh, it's beautiful," Lindsey remarked, as she looked out over the ocean as the sun dipped below the horizon. The gentle ocean breeze blew her hair and the sounds of the waves crashing resonated in the background.

"Yes, it is," Harris remarked. "Something about this place just warms my heart, you know?"

"I know … it's almost magical in a way." She speared a tomato wedge with her fork and popped it in her mouth.

"Did I mention to you how stunning you look tonight?" he asked suddenly.

"Um, no," she said uncertainly, caught off guard.

"Well, you do," he replied matter-of-factly before beginning to cut his steak.

"Thanks, Harris," she said with a small smile, warmed by his compliment, or maybe the wine—she wasn't sure.

They chatted easily over dinner—Harris kept her fascinated as he described his latest plot idea for his next thriller, and he seemed truly interested in her fast-paced day-to-day life in New York, asking her a bunch of questions about her job, her neighborhood, and her favorite restaurants.

"I'm sure you're wondering why I keep peppering you with so many questions about the city," he said before drinking the last bit of wine in his glass.

"A little," she answered truthfully.

"I'm considering a move to New York this fall. I've been offered a teaching position at NYU, and I don't think I can pass it up," he confided.

"Wow, that's awesome, Harris." She stared at her dinner companion, and she wasn't sure if it was the rather large glass of wine, the beauty of the evening or the fact that she finally felt truly happy for the first time since … the happenings of the previous week, but she saw Harris with a new set of eyes. Seated across from her was an incredibly handsome best-selling author that made her laugh with his witty quips and dry humor. She also felt strangely proud of him and his accomplishments, perhaps because he was Kate's brother and she'd known bits and pieces of his struggle and his story to get to where he was today.

"Thanks, Lindsey," he smiled back at her, and she felt a little tingle, a moment where everything around Harris grew hazy and she could only focus on the intense, yet dreamy, look in his eyes. She shook her head, darted her eyes away. It was the wine. It had to be the wine.

She jumped up and grabbed her plate from the table.

"Finished?" She asked, her voice too high-pitched, too sugary. She inwardly winced at the sound.

"Yes, but you don't have to—"

"Oh, I don't mind," she replied, taking his plate along with hers and rushing inside. She deposited the dirty plates in the sink and put her hands on the sides of the sink, her eyes focusing on a wayward lettuce leaf stuck to the pale blue china.

Breathe in, breathe out, she told herself. *And stop drinking so much!* her conscience added. It was no big deal to have a moment of attraction for someone else. Especially someone as good-looking and admirable as Harris. It didn't mean that she would act on the impulse or anything.

A throat cleared behind her. "Everything alright, Lindsey?"

She whirled around, pasting a smile in place as she nodded too vigorously. "Yes, perfect. The wine just," she fanned herself, "whew, got to me, you know? Is it warm in here?" she asked, moving to begin putting away the rest of the cooking supplies still lingering on the countertop.

Harris appeared thoughtful. "Not really. Are you sure you're feeling alright? We can take a rain check for our big night out," he told her with a wink.

"No way! We are going to have so much fun—and I promise—I'm fine. I think I just need some water."

She crossed the kitchen to the fridge and pulled out a bottle of spring water, opened it and took a big gulp. The frigid liquid coursed into her core, shocking her system and countering the effects of the wine. She could do this. She was going to be fine and she would rein in her wayward feelings, too.

Three hours later, Lindsey decided she was certainly not having fun. Maybe she was getting too old for crazy nights out in loud, obnoxious bars filled with even louder, obnoxious drunk people. The bar was noisy and filled with smoke and she'd been hit on by enough skeevy guys to form a baseball team. She shuddered.

She glanced to her left where Harris stood, looking about as excited as she did. Right in front of them, a couple who could only barely be old enough to get in the bar made out ravenously. She wrinkled her nose and Harris turned to her. They shared a disgusted look.

"It's like a train wreck—so terrible, but I can't look away," she said as the couple got ridiculously handsy.

"Ready to go?" he asked.

"Absolutely," she replied. He reached for her hand, and she gave it to him, too excited at the feel of it, even though surely he only held her hand so that they wouldn't lose track of one another in the overly crowded bar.

Back at the beach house, Lindsey immediately slipped her feet out of the four-inch heels she wore. "Ahh, that feels good," she said, stretching her toes.

"Why do you wear them if they hurt so much?" Harris asked, seeming truly curious.

"Because, they make me taller and improve my posture."

"It's not because they make your legs look killer?" he asked, his eyebrow arched.

"Okay, maybe that, too," she relented. She started up the steps. "I'm going to shower off and pray the god-awful scent of cigarette smoke will come out of my hair with just one shampoo," she complained. "Goodnight, Harris," she added over her shoulder.

"Goodnight, Lindsey. Sleep well." She looked back to see him smiling up at her in a way that made her insides feel mushy and her heart grow strangely tight in her chest. She smiled goofily back, but turned and shook her head as she continued up the stairs. What in the world was happening here? Not something she had planned for, that was for sure.

Chapter 4

She inhaled the tantalizing scent of bacon cooking before she'd even opened her eyes the morning following their failed attempt at bar-hopping. Lindsey stretched and yawned in the huge, fluffy bed, luxuriating in the feel of the Egyptian cotton on her softer than normal skin. The sand and sea were doing wonders with their exfoliating powers.

Hopping out of the bed with more energy than she'd had in days, she pulled her hair into a messy bun and made her way downstairs, still wearing her tank top and ruffled pajama shorts. She found Harris at the stove making what smelled like a delicious breakfast.

"Smells good in here," she said in greeting. He turned briefly to nod at her.

"Coffee?" He asked.

"Don't mind if I do," she said, pulling a mug with bright flowers splashed all over it from the glass-paned cabinet. "Did you sleep well?" she asked politely.

"I sure did. You?"

"Absolutely." She poured her coffee, found some cream in the fridge for it. "Need any help?"

"Nah, I'm about finished. Hope you like pancakes because this recipe made way more than I thought it would."

"I love them—who doesn't?"

Lindsey set the table and poured them each a glass of orange juice while Harris finished cooking. While he transferred the pancakes to a plate, she rummaged in the pantry for maple syrup.

"So what's your plan for the day?" she asked once they'd sat down to eat.

"I'm going to spend the morning working, but I hope to hit the beach for a little while this afternoon."

"Nice."

"What about you?"

"No real plan—tanning, reading, napping ... you know, the usual for a typical Thursday," she shrugged.

"Care to join me at the beach later?"

"I'd love to join you. It's always nice to nap and tan beside someone," she teased.

He gave her a pointed look. "I hope you're up for some time in the ocean. I can't just lie there in the sand all afternoon," he told her.

"I'm up for anything," she said, surprising herself with her flirty-sounding words.

Harris arched an eyebrow at her.

"Oh, you know what I mean." She wagged a finger and shook her head at him.

"Do I?"

"Oh my gosh, I'm leaving now," she said with mock exaggeration. She rolled her eyes, but an amused smile stayed on her lips long after she'd left the kitchen. On her way to change for the beach, she found herself hoping the next few hours would pass by quickly.

Thanks to a nice, long nap beneath a navy-and-white striped umbrella, her hope paid off. The time passed quickly and before she knew it, she glanced up from her magazine to see Harris crossing over the dunes. Happy to see him, she shut the slick pages of *Glamour* and hopped up, waving excitedly.

"Hey! Long time, no see, stranger!" she called out.

He tossed his head back and laughed like a carefree kid. Something inside Lindsey warmed at the sight of him—his wavy hair blowing in the wind, his eyes closed against the bright sun as the sound of his laughter carried on the breeze.

"I always imagined you to be quiet and studious," she told him when he reached the two beach chairs she'd set out for them.

"Linds, we were around each other, like no joke, twice before yesterday."

"Yes, and both times you were very quiet."

"My Gran's funeral and yours and Kate's graduation ceremony weren't the best places for conversation opportunities, you have to admit."

"I wasn't counting graduation."

"What other time did we see each other?" he asked, knitting his brow as he racked his memory.

"It was here at the beach—the summer after mine and Kate's freshman year. But I'm not surprised you don't remember meeting me. You were too busy sucking face with that snobby redhead," she said, swatting his shoulder playfully.

He rolled his eyes. "Oh God, Shea. Now I remember—she was the worst. I can't believe I even brought her to our family get-together that year. And you're right, she really was a snob."

Lindsey studied him for a moment before asking her next question. "Why haven't you been around that much the past few years? I'm pretty sure I've been present at more of your family's events than you have," she pointed out.

"Ouch, that's harsh, but true. I've just been busy—writing is a solitary craft that takes up most of my time."

"Yes, but you have to live life to write about it, don't you?"

"You would be surprised how handy a tool the internet can be. Cuts out the whole having to go out and explore necessity. Makes one much more efficient and requires less talking to people."

"Or it makes the process way lamer and super boring."

"Hey, but in my defense, I'm spending next week with my family, and you actually don't come to every family thing—I always come home for Thanksgiving and Christmas," he informed her.

"Yeah, I have my own family I have to visit sometimes, you know," she replied sarcastically.

Harris glanced out toward the waves where they crashed loudly along the shoreline. "So are we going to go for a swim or what?" he asked.

"Beat you there!" Lindsey sang, dashing across the hot sand. Harris quickly caught up with her, but instead of passing her to win the impromptu race, he scooped her up in his arms instead.

"No!" she squealed, laughing as she struggled against his tight hold. He ran with her right into the surf, offering Lindsey no chance for escape before he dipped them both under water, still holding onto her. Seconds later, she came up, gasping and swatting at him.

"That was such a cheap shot!" She gasped for air, saltwater in her mouth.

Harris shook his head, sending water droplets in every direction. "I saw a chance, and I took it," he defended, shrugging his shoulders.

Lindsey narrowed her eyes at him, not giving him a chance to recover before pushing him over in the waist-deep water. Laughing, she watched him regain his balance and mock-scowl at her.

"I feel better now that we are even," she explained with her own little shrug.

He grabbed her around the waist, meaning to pull her back down, but the mocking smile on his face fell when she threw her arms around him. She'd locked her hands around him not only to steady herself, but also as an act of defense—if she went down he was going down with her—however, in the brief seconds of pause, the fleeting hesitation when she glanced up at him as his smile turned serious, her breath had hitched and everything between them changed.

The moment was no longer a joke. Tight against his bare chest, his arms snaked securely around her waist, just above her bikini bottom, things had turned intense in the blink of an eye. He stared down at her, clearly facing the same internal struggle that she did as his eyes smoldered, burning deep into her very core.

She could no longer think rationally as excitement and desire for him clouded her mind. As the waves rocked gently around them, they clung to one another, forgetting all else. Nothing but the man in front of her mattered. Lindsey was suddenly very aware that she'd never wanted anything more than she wanted him to kiss her at that exact moment. Was he going to kiss her? She couldn't tell if he would actually make the move or not. He appeared as though he wanted to, but something might have been holding him back. Her eyes drifted to his lips as she lifted her face towards his to encourage him.

Harris looked down at the lovely girl in his arms as a war raged mightily within him. He didn't want to let her go—ever. It felt right to have her in his arms. He wanted to kiss her, toss her over his shoulder and take her inside the house and …

But she'd been engaged last week—he kept trying to internally shout that fact as want and desire rapidly overpowered his mind. This wasn't going to end well. He needed to be her friend. Just her friend. That was all. But why did it have to feel so good to have her in his arms? Or to laugh with her over the dumbest jokes? Or to share a meal with her and linger as the conversation never ended?

When she tilted her face towards him, giving her silent permission, the battle was over. It was clear that they both wanted this. He leaned down and brushed his lips against hers, but just barely, gently testing the waters, making sure that it was right.

She pressed her soft lips firm against his, and his blood quickened. Giving in to the impulse, he intensified his kiss, pulling her even tighter against him as her fingers tangled into his wet hair. She tasted salty like the sea, and warm like the bright sun overhead. With the tide tugging against them, she wrapped her weightless legs around his waist as he ground his feet into the shifting sand beneath them.

They eagerly clung to one another as the kiss exploded into a myriad of fireworks. As his tongue found hers, she moaned softly and his hands began to roam lower, pulling her closer, but it would never be close enough.

So enrapt in kissing Lindsey, he didn't see the gigantic wave coming, didn't feel it until the force was already knocking them both over and under the waves. His mouth and nose filled with seawater as Lindsey let go of him and pushed herself toward the surface. He followed immediately and they both came up, coughing and sputtering.

What was he supposed to do? He very well couldn't yank her back in his arms and continue where they'd left off before the wave had so rudely interrupted them. The air now hung awkwardly between them.

Lindsey cleared her throat. "I think … it's getting too warm out. I—I had better head inside," she said, already swiftly heading toward the shore. He barely had a chance to nod before she'd moved even further away from him. He watched as she reached the sand and grabbed up her towel. She tossed it around her and ran for the house like a bee was after her.

Still stunned as the waves lapped around him, he attempted to process what had just happened between them. They'd kissed. Boy, had they just kissed. His heart still thudded from the electricity surging through his veins from when he'd had her in his arms, his lips on hers. As amazing as it was, the kiss had changed everything though. He had to eventually go back into the house. What were they supposed to do now?

Chapter 5

The steady stream of hot water did little to clear her desire-muddled thoughts. Lindsey stood in a disbelieving daze under the rainfall showerhead as the glass doors clouded over with a thick layer of steam. She'd kissed Harris! Why had she kissed him? Now everything had changed!

She pressed her fingers against her swollen lips, remembering how her blood had sizzled when their lips first met, how she clung to him, craving more, wanting to be as close to him as possible, unable to be satisfied. He stirred feelings in her she hadn't thought it was possible to experience—not even with Patrick.

But Harris was Kate's brother! And she'd only just ended a very serious relationship not even an entire week ago. There were dozens of reasons why hooking up with Harris was an all-around bad idea. But then she remembered how well they got along, how much they laughed when they were together, how it felt like they'd been close friends for years rather than just a couple of days. Throwing in their amazing kiss in the ocean, and her heart certainly teetered toward having a serious case of the feels for him.

Lindsey sighed dreamily every time she closed her eyes and remembered how it felt—the waves against her bare skin, his hands all over her, his mouth devouring hers. She couldn't pretend it didn't happen—no matter how hard she'd tried in the past half hour. But could she bring it up with him? Her cheeks reddened at the thought. Maybe, it was best to act as if nothing was any different between them.

She turned off the water and stepped into the foggy bathroom. After drying off, she put on a strapless jersey dress and braided her wet hair, pulling the long, thick fishtail braid neatly over her shoulder. With her hand on her bedroom door, she figured it was time to face the music. Seeing Harris was inevitable—and the way she'd just run from him had her cheeks burning with embarrassment. Who knew what would it would be like once they faced each other? Her stomach was in knots at the thought.

Downstairs, the house was still and quiet. She could have heard a pin drop. As she made herself a cup of coffee, she wondered if he'd made his way back in from the beach yet. Lindsey took her coffee into the cozy living room and flipped on the television. *Mystic Pizza* was featured on Netflix, so she settled in with her coffee to watch it, feeling snuggly with her bare feet stretched out on the sofa and a warm mug in her hands.

A third of the way into the movie, the back door opened, startling Lindsey, despite the fact that she had been listening for Harris' arrival since the moment she'd headed downstairs after taking a shower. She popped her head over the back of the slipcovered sofa as he tossed his towel carelessly by the back door. When he turned to head upstairs, he saw her staring at him, wide-eyed. So much for acting like nothing had happened.

"I'm going to shower, and then we're going to talk," he said, brief but serious. She nodded her agreement solemnly before he headed up the staircase. Just fifteen minutes later, Harris returned, freshly showered and dressed in navy shorts and T-shirt. Lindsey paused the movie as Harris took a seat on the opposite end of the sofa. Neither of them looked at the other, nor did they speak for what felt like an eternity.

Finally, Harris was the one to break the silence. "Lindsey, what happened out there ..." he trailed off.

"I know. I'm sorry—I guess I was so caught up in the moment, I wasn't thinking clearly, and it didn't dawn on me the weight of what we were doing," she explained rapidly, her heart fluttering.

"Neither did I. That moment that led to our kiss caught me totally off guard, but I can't sit here and say I'm sorry that it happened, Lindsey."

"But it makes everything weird between us," she said, fiddling with the hem of her dress.

"It doesn't have to make things weird."

Lindsey turned to him, leaning forward. "Harris, it's weird right now."

He leaned closer to her. "I'm telling you, it doesn't have to be," he said softly.

"How can we make it go back to before? There's no way—everything has changed."

"Yes, it has. But is that such a bad thing?" he asked, searching her eyes as he waited for her response.

"There's so many reasons why this," she gestured between the two of them, "is a bad idea. You're my best friend's brother, and I just went through a terrible breakup. Besides, we barely know each other," she numbered the reasons off on her fingers.

"Out there in the ocean, when I had you in my arms, did it seem like being together was a bad idea?"

She swallowed hard. "I couldn't think straight out there," she admitted.

"Neither could I, but didn't it feel nice not to think for a minute? Just to feel? I've never felt more alive than I did out there, Lindsey."

"Me, either," she admitted, her voice barely above a whisper.

He reached out and caressed her cheek. "Then let's just see what happens between us. We have these few days with just the two of us here ..."

"I'm not that type of girl, Harris. I don't have one-night stands or randomly hook up with men."

"I don't either, Lindsey, especially that second part you mention," he said, lightening the tension, "and I hope you don't consider what I'm suggesting to be either of those things. I care about you—you're Kate's closest friend and I would never do anything to hurt you. I just want to spend time with you. I really like you."

Lindsey stared at him, felt the intensity of his gaze on her, those gorgeous eyes of his searching her own, waiting patiently for her to answer. His thumb lightly traced a pattern back and forth across her cheek, causing tingles to shoot down her spine in the most delicious way.

"I'm up for spending some time together," she told him, the words popping almost involuntarily from her mouth.

He drew even closer to her until he was mere inches from her face. "I forgot to mention—kissing. Kissing definitely has to be involved in our time together," he smiled as his eyes drifted to her lips.

"I think I can be okay with that," she said just before he captured her mouth with his own. All other thoughts and hesitations floated away as his kiss burned through her. Her heart quickened, and heat pooled deep within her as she leaned toward him, unable to get enough of the flames he fanned inside of her. He kissed her like she was the very breath he needed to survive and he couldn't dare let her go. As his lips molded against hers, he wrapped his arms around her, running them up and down in a tantalizing pattern firmly against her back.

She sighed in pleasure when his lips broke away from hers and he buried his face in the hollow of her neck. His five-o'clock shadow scraped deliciously against the sensitive skin at the base of her throat as he planted kisses in a row along her collarbone. She kept arching back as the sensations he created intensified until her head rested against throw pillows and she was lying on the sofa, Harris practically on top of her.

The pressure of his firm body, the luxury of his kisses and the constant flow of words of adoration he whispered between them—"You're beautiful," "You taste like sunshine," and "I never want to stop kissing you," to name but a few—was like a drug, one to which she was quickly becoming addicted. But as his hand drifted down to her bare leg and started making its way back up, inching slowly along her thigh and beneath the hem of her already hitched up dress, she froze.

"We're not going to just be kissing much longer, are we?" she breathed as she placed her hand on top of his to stop its ascension and to slow them down, even if for but a few seconds.

He leaned back from where he'd been kissing along the top swells of her breasts, contemplating her question. "Do you want to stop? We can stop. Whatever you want, Linds. The last thing in the world I would want to do is push you," he said, sounding strained though he emphasized his last few words.

She shook her head. "I don't want to stop," she admitted, "but I don't know if I'm ready for how this really will change things. I mean, a kiss is one thing … but, sleeping together …" She trailed off, their heavy breathing the only sound in the room.

"It doesn't have to change anything," he said as he leaned over her and kissed her cheek. "I want you, God knows I do, but I respect you too much to have you right now," he said, sitting up. The air around her suddenly felt cool. She missed his closeness, his warmth.

"I didn't say stop," she complained.

"I don't want to be a part of something you'll regret," he told her and stood up to stretch. She watched him, stunned.

"You're seriously putting the brakes on this right now?" she asked, astounded.

"Yep. Ready to get dinner started?" he asked matter-of-factly before turning and heading to the kitchen. Lindsey watched him leave, her brain still foggy and her heart still beating faster than if she'd just completed a half-marathon. He was right about one thing—he was a part of something she regretted. She was full on regretting opening her mouth about stopping the steamy connection they'd shared mere seconds earlier...

She jumped up and followed him to the kitchen where he was rummaging in the fridge.

"Harris."

He looked over and closed the refrigerator. "Hmm?" he asked.

"I'm not hungry."

"By the time we get dinner finished, I'm sure you will be. It's nearing seven as it is."

She stepped over to where he stood, a package of chicken in his hand. She took the chicken and stuck it back in the fridge before taking his hand and leading him from the kitchen.

"Where are we ... oh." He followed her lead as she held his hand and pulled him up the steps and down the hall to the big bedroom with its luxurious bed and windows that opened to the ocean.

She let go of his hand as soon as they'd entered her bedroom and wrapped her arms around his neck.

"You're sure about this?" Harris asked, searching her eyes as he put his hands around her waist.

She nodded slowly, her eyes never breaking away from his gaze. "Very sure," she whispered before kissing him soundly. His hands slid down her waist, continuing on, running to the backs of her legs before going back up and cupping her bottom firmly, pulling her against his growing hardness.

The movement stirred a ravenous hunger within her and she tightened her grasp around him as he walked them over to the bed. She took the hem of her dress in her hands, about to throw it off, but he placed his hands over hers to stop her.

"I'll undress you in a minute, Lindsey," he said, his voice low. All she could do was nod as she released her grip on the soft fabric. His hands didn't grab hold of the dress, but instead, slid beneath it along the sides of her upper thighs. They slowly crept upward, past the lace of her panties to her waist before going back down, beneath the lace, edging her panties down her legs. He helped her step out of the scrap of white lace before tossing it across the room. Her breath came in quick little puffs as she stood, mesmerized and completely under his spell, aching to know what would be coming next.

Pressing her legs against the soft white quilt, he gently pushed her down onto the bed. Her dress slid up to the very top of her legs. In an act of flirty defiance, she slid her hands down and up her legs, the dress beneath them coming along for the journey up to her waist. Harris stared down at her as she bared herself, sucking in a sharp breath. Tossing his shirt over his head, he leaned over her, pressing a kiss to her lips. She arched her hips against him, loving his kisses, but past ready for his hands to be on her body.

"I want you so bad," she panted, half-crazed for the man who had yet to even caress her intimately.

He kissed along the edge of her strapless dress before tugging it down, freeing her breasts. As he cupped her breast in his hand, she arched her back, pressing her nipple into his palm, craving his touch. He obliged her, running his thumb back and forth along the taut bud before leaning down and teasing it with his tongue. She moaned as a deep yearning ached within her.

His hand continued down her body, stopping to slide between her legs. She opened to him, silently begging for more. She'd never been driven this crazy with desire in her entire life. Whether it was the beach, the carefree attitude she'd tried to adopt, or just the excellent, take-charge sexiness Harris exuded in the bedroom, she wasn't sure, and at the moment, she didn't care.

"Tell me what you want, Lindsey," he said as his hand moved skillfully on her most intimate place.

"You know what I want," she moaned, pressing against him, seeking relief from the intense throbbing he was slowly building within her.

"Do I?" he asked softly, taking his hand away. She pushed herself onto her elbows to see him unbuttoning his shorts, the zipper coming down. She watched as he slid them off, revealing his long, hard cock. Seconds later, he came over her, and she felt him pressing against her, barely able to contain his steady control, wanting to be inside of her as badly as she wanted it, too.

"Tell me what you want," he repeated, hovering over her. She arched her hips upward, wanting him badly.

"I want you inside of me," she breathed impatiently, squirming beneath him. He'd pushed her to the edge and drawn her back more times than she cared for— she wanted, no she needed, a release.

"Why?" he asked, and even through the haze of desire, she wanted to hit him.

"What do you want me to say?" she asked, half-crazed.

"Whatever you want to say," he said, still so in control.

"I don't want to talk. I want to feel. You inside me— thrusting, moving, losing yourself," she said, surprising herself with how turned on she was by her own words.

"That's it," he said as he slid inside of her in one deep thrust. She yelped at the intense, hot sweetness of it. Once it began, it was relentless, pulsing and pounding in a rhythm she could barely contain. She cried out as the first waves of ecstasy violently shattered within her and around her, and he followed soon after her, finding his own release before they collapsed into a sweaty heap on the still made bed.

"Wow ... Harris ... just ... wow," Lindsey sighed a few moments later when she could finally breathe again.

He propped himself on his elbows and smiled down at her. "Wow, yourself," he replied.

"You didn't give me a chance ... you just took over and ... blew my mind."

"I think you needed a little mind-blowing."

"I appreciate that. I think I did, too," she laughed. It felt good to laugh, and strangely odd, seeing that they were on top of her covers, mostly naked and post-lovemaking. Her stomach rumbled.

"I thought you said you weren't hungry."

"I wasn't, but I guess I worked up an appetite," she explained with a shrug.

"I'm starved," he said, and with a quick kiss to her forehead, he hopped up and walked splendidly naked to the bathroom. Lindsey took the opportunity to stand and straighten her dress back out. Catching a glimpse in the mirror, she quickly tossed it over her head and shrugged on her robe. There was no way to salvage the rumpled dress.

"Nice robe," Harris remarked as he emerged from the bathroom and grabbed his shorts.

"Thanks," she replied, smoothing her hands over the crisp, white cotton.

"Did you want to make dinner or go out tonight?" he asked, locating his shirt from where it had been tossed carelessly in the corner of the room.

She stretched. "I think I'd rather stay in. You?"

He smiled knowingly at her. "Staying in sounds like a good plan to me."

"Do you want to go ahead and start making dinner while I get dressed?"

"Sounds like a plan," he said, coming to her and planting a quick kiss on her lips and smiling down at her. "See you downstairs in a few."

After Harris left, she rummaged through her suitcase to find something else to wear, all the while her mind reeling. They'd just slept together! What was this? Was it a way to rebound from her heartbreak? If so, Harris wasn't the best candidate for that job. Sure, he was sexy as hell, intelligent, successful, funny, they'd just had the most amazing sex of her life … the list went on and on. But he was Kate's brother. That made things complicated. She sighed as she pulled on a tank top and yoga pants. Too late now. Best to keep things light and casual and just enjoy one another. It certainly would keep her mind off what had happened with Patrick at least.

Chapter 6

Harris chopped red peppers with an intensity and vigor he'd never possessed for a common kitchen task. What had he done? What had he been thinking? Why had he let his heart overpower his mind? He knew better than to let the insane chemistry between him and Lindsey go this far. Lindsey was Kate's best friend, and she had just gone through an awful breakup. That meant she should've been off-limits. If he had even half a brain, he wouldn't have slept with her.

Sliding the strips of pepper into a bowl, he mentally kicked himself. If it hadn't been for that mind-melding kiss at the beach he could have kept his distance. He could've admired her from afar. He enjoyed her company immensely, she was beautiful inside and out with a sense of humor to boot. The perfect girl. It was hard enough to focus on the editing he'd originally planned on handling this week, but now it would be harder than ever to resist her, and truthfully, he didn't think he wanted to anymore. Maybe it wasn't the smartest decision to begin something with her, but he couldn't help it. He was falling for her. He just had to keep things light, simple. No one needed to get hurt.

As he looked through the cabinets for a pan to sauté the pepper strips, Lindsey appeared, looking relaxed and radiant in her simple top and pants. Her skin, kissed by the sun, practically glowed and a soft, contented smile played on her lips. She'd managed to smooth out the braid that had grown tangled during their ... time together.

"Need any help?" she asked, approaching the counter.

"You can shred the cheese if you'd like," he said, gesturing to a block of Monterey Jack and the cheese grater he'd set out on the countertop.

While she grated, he sautéed—seasoned chicken in one pan, peppers and onions in another—and neither really said much, both simply focusing on their tasks.

"Mmm, it's smelling so good in here," Lindsey remarked. Finished with the cheese, she began slicing avocados. "I think I need to whip up a batch of margaritas to go with these fajitas," she added.

"That sounds like a great idea," Harris agreed, tossing the vegetables and chicken together.

Once they'd finished cooking dinner, they carried their plates outside to eat at "their" table by the pool. Lindsey pulled out her phone and selected a station that played Latin and salsa music to coordinate with their dinner.

"Festive," Harris quipped, taking a sip of his drink, realizing it contained mostly tequila and very little margarita mix.

"Cheesy?" Lindsey asked, scrunching her nose as she waited for his response.

"As hell, but I like it," he said with a wink, making her laugh. He loved to hear her laugh.

They talked and teased one another, laughing and lingering over dinner until the sky was completely dark and full of stars glittering above them. Their evening together couldn't have gone any more perfectly.

"I guess it's getting late," she said, trying to stifle a yawn.

"Tired?" he asked, leaning back in his chair.

"Not terribly so. I was actually thinking about going for a moonlight swim," she said, her voice soft and lilting.

He arched an eyebrow at her suggestive words.

"Right now," she added, standing and walking the few steps to the edge of the lighted pool, her tank top coming over her head and drifting to the natural stone decking. He certainly didn't mind watching as she shimmied out of her yoga pants and promptly slipped gracefully into the water, turning around and beckoning for him to join her impromptu skinny dipping.

Seconds later, he jumped none too elegantly into the heated water. "So, you're really into skinny dipping, huh?" he joked, swimming close to her.

She laughed. "Only when it's dark outside." She splashed him.

His glance fell below the surface of the crystal-clear water lit by several lights scattered along the pool's walls. "Well, I, for one, enjoy the view," he said, drawing up next to her and pulling her against him. He kissed her gently, then waited to gage her response.

"Harris," she whispered his name between their kisses, "I'm so glad we ended up here all alone together," she added as his lips moved down her neck. She sighed breathily.

"Me, too," he responded before completely losing himself in the moment, but not without taking her with him every step of the way.

***

The next morning, Lindsey's eyes slowly cracked open and she reached out across her bed, fully expecting to feel Harris' warm body beside her, but the cool crispness of the cotton sheets was the only thing beneath her hand. She frowned in disappointment, despite the pleasant memory of falling asleep in his arms still lingering in her mind. Where had he gotten off to so early in the morning? Did he already regret spending the night in her room? Were things getting too intense too fast for him? Tons of conflicting thoughts played back and forth in her mind within a matter of minutes. She was certainly awake now. And curious.

She threw on her short, ruffled robe and tiptoed through the silent house. The sun was barely up and the hall was still very dim. She peeked inside the guest room in which he normally took up residence while staying at the beach house, but he wasn't there. She managed to make her way downstairs and that's when she caught a glimpse of him outside, seated in a lounge chair with a cup of coffee in his hand.

"A little early to be catching rays," she said in greeting as she stepped onto the patio. The morning air was a little cool with the breeze coming off the ocean rather steadily.

"Good morning to you, too," he said back to her, setting the thick stack of papers he held down on the table next to him.

"It's really early." She crossed her arms across her body to ward off the chill.

"I'm an early riser. I didn't disturb you, did I?"

"No, not at all. I just wondered where you had gone, that's all."

"I came out to watch the sunrise and try to get at least a little bit of work done," he explained to her.

Lindsey nodded as she perched on the edge of the chair beside him. "Harris, we need to talk."

"You're right, we do." He sighed.

"What's happening between us is happening so fast," she started carefully.

"I know it is, but," Harris paused to take Lindsey's hand in his, "doesn't it feel so right? So good?"

She squeezed his hand. "It really does," she admitted.

He tugged at her hand and the motion pulled her down from her perch and onto his lap. He wrapped his arms around her, kissing her tousled hair. "I went through all the pros and cons, too. But, at the end of the day … or rather, at the beginning, you in my arms just feels right. That's all that matters, don't you think?"

Lindsey stared out at the ocean as the sun began to peep just above the horizon while he held her close and secure. She soaked in the words he'd said and what they meant. Nothing in her life, despite all her previous attempts at careful planning and order, had ever felt as right as the very simple, spontaneous moment with Harris she was sharing right then. She fleetingly thought how nice it would be to wake up with him every morning, for him to be the first person she spoke with each day, but then she quickly shoved the betraying notion away. No matter how right it felt, she needed to keep things between them as casual as possible for both of their sakes.

They spent the most perfect of beach days lounging in the sun, walking hand-in-hand along the packed sand at the ocean's edge, randomly heading to the beach house to make love, and never venturing all that far from one another's side. To Lindsey, her time with Harris felt good and right, like a dream from which she never wanted to wake, and as she fell asleep tucked safely in his arms, she wanted nothing more than for the moments she shared with him to last forever.

But all too soon, one day blissfully faded into another and their week was coming to a close. The day had arrived for Lindsey to pack up and head back to New York. That morning, she woke with a frown on her face.

"What's wrong, sweetie?" Harris asked in a hushed tone, his lips against her bare shoulder as the morning light streamed softly into the bedroom. She could hear the sounds of the waves crashing in the distance from where they'd left the windows open.

"Your family is coming in tomorrow—I've got to go home today, face the real world again," she explained, not liking the words she was saying one little bit.

"No, you don't," he smiled against her neck, pulling her close. "Stay—it's a holiday week anyway and it's not like you'll be all that busy at work. Besides, you know my family loves you—you don't need to go anywhere," he told her.

"I don't know, Harris. It might be kind of weird," she said slowly, though his suggestion to extend her beach stay was incredibly tempting. She had tons of vacation time at work, and he was right, nothing much would be going on during the holiday week.

"We can keep what's going on between us a secret. No one has to know about us. Just stay. Please. I know Mom and Dad think of you like an extra daughter, and how happy would it make you to spend some time at the beach with Kate?" He made an awfully tempting case.

"You do have a point …"

"Not to mention, how fun would it be to sneak around like two teenagers, trying not to get caught?" His hand roamed down her body, and she closed her eyes and sighed dreamily, imagining secret rendezvous with Harris on the beach, in the shower, in his room … the list could go on forever.

"You've convinced me. I'll stay through the Fourth. Fireworks at the beach are too fabulous to pass up anyway."

"You can move your stuff into the room next to mine before the cleaning crew comes today to make things easier, but for now, how about we create our own little fireworks show?" he asked, tossing back the bedcovers and positioning himself on top of her. She welcomed him enthusiastically, her hands gliding along the sinews of his shoulders and back, more content than she ever imagined she could possibly be.

Chapter 7

"LINDSEYYY!" Kate squealed in excitement as she dropped a pile of her bags onto the front foyer's floor. Kate threw her arms around her best friend and jumped up and down in excitement. "It's been way too long since we've been at the beach together!"

"Kate," Lindsey laughed, "We were just here Memorial Day weekend not even two months ago, but I'm happy to be at the beach with you, too!"

"You look refreshed and happy," Kate said conspiratorially, linking her arm through Lindsey's as they walked towards the back of the house.

"I am," Lindsey admitted, but quickly changed the subject. "Everyone's out back by the pool, but do you want me to help you get all of your luggage upstairs? I don't mind."

"Nah, I'll get them taken care of later. Let's go outside! I can't wait to see everyone! Especially Harris—can you believe we haven't seen each other since Christmas?"

They headed out the French doors and Kate squealed again when she saw her big brother, who promptly hopped up and hurried over to his little sister, scooping her up into a big bear hug.

"It's been too long, Kate!" Harris said, giving her a sound kiss on the cheek.

"I know, bro! So what've you been up to? Writing the latest and greatest American novel?" she asked, punching his arm.

"If you consider mystery thrillers that go straight to paperback profound American literature, then I am in the process of the greatest literary accomplishment of my life," he joked.

"Ha-ha, very funny. We all know your books always hit the bestsellers list. But I like your attempt at a joke," she kidded with him.

"Kate, Lindsey, Harris, come sit and have a glass of Chardonnay with us," Gina Welling called out from the comfy outdoor sectional situated on the patio to provide panoramic views of the ocean. She and her husband, Howard, along with their other daughter Melanie and her husband, Jonathan, were lounging with their drinks, not a care in the world but to enjoy the day and each other's company.

The trio made their way over to where the rest of the family was seated, and Harris poured Lindsey and Kate a glass of wine before taking his own glass back up again. He made sure to situate himself beside Lindsey when they all took their seats.

"So, has the weather been this wonderful all week?" Gina asked, looking at Lindsey and Harris.

"Yes, it's been gorgeous," Lindsey said, sipping the crisp, fruity wine.

"It was hard to get much work done with this awesome weather and the perfect waves just outside the door," Harris admitted.

"I thought you looked much more tan than normal," Kate remarked. "When did you get here, Harris?"

"I came down from Portland last Tuesday."

"Oh, I'm surprised you didn't call me and tell me that, Lindsey," Kate said, looking between the two seated beside one another. Lindsey could see her mind working, trying to figure out why she hadn't been kept in the loop.

"I was going to leave, but Harris insisted that I stay, and we've actually had a pretty good time hanging out and stuff," Lindsey said, smiling as she casually shrugged.

"Well, Lindsey, we were all so sorry to hear about you and Patrick," Melanie said sympathetically.

Lindsey swallowed, surprised that they knew about what had happened, seeing as she'd kept it under wraps. Kate must've explained to her parents why she'd needed to come down to the beach early and they'd told Melanie. "It's okay, it was probably for the best actually," she said with a resolute nod, certainly not wanting to go into details.

"I'm glad that you finally see that, Linds," Kate replied. "You know I was never a Patrick fan. He had the worst sense of style and his jokes were so not even close to funny." Kate laughed, picking up her own glass of wine.

"I can always count on you for your honest opinion," Lindsey remarked drily.

***

Later that evening, Harris snuck into Lindsey's room while she was getting ready for dinner. Gina had made reservations at the 1770 House for all of them.

"I miss you," he said, pulling her into his arms.

"We were together all day today," she replied, confused. She set the brush she'd been using down on the dresser and threw her arms around his neck, kissing him soundly.

"It's not the same," he said, kissing her neck.

"Okay, maybe you're right," she conceded, surrendering to his kisses.

"I knew it!" Kate exclaimed out of nowhere.

Lindsey turned in Harris' arms to see her best friend's silhouette in the doorway. Her eyes were wide in shock, her cheeks bright red. They hadn't heard her approach.

"You've caught us," Harris admitted good-naturedly, not letting go of Lindsey.

"I'll say I did. How long has this been going on?" Kate asked, gesturing to the two of them still locked in their cozy embrace.

Harris and Lindsey shared a glance.

"Since last Wednesday?" Lindsey ventured, eyebrows raised.

Kate nearly choked. "Last Wednesday!? You guys both got here last Tuesday! You two sure didn't waste any time, did you?"

Lindsey broke away from Harris and took a few steps over to Kate. She turned to Harris and said, "I think it's best if I talk to Kate by myself for a minute to explain things between us a little better." He nodded and scooted around them to get out of Lindsey's room.

"Lindsey!" Kate cried when the door shut behind them.

"I know what you're thinking, but it's not like that."

"Really? You're not rebounding with my brother of all people?"

"No. He isn't a rebound. I really like him. A lot. I honestly could see something amazing happening between us, Kate, and I would never treat him like just some random guy that can help me forget about Patrick. He's important to you, and therefore, he is, and will always be, important to me. That's all beside the fact that I think I'm falling head over heels for him," she told Kate.

Kate contemplated Lindsey's heartfelt confession for a moment before she spoke again. "Wow, if you really like him, then I'm honestly very happy for the two of you. There's no one in the world I could have picked that would be better for either of you guys than one another now that I think about it, and of course, I love you both so much," she relented, but then she issued a warning. "But you had better not hurt him, Linds."

"I promise, I won't. I'm surprised and excited by what's happening between us, and to tell you the truth, I'm kind of glad you figured it out because I've wanted to tell you about him so bad!"

"I bet! I'm kind of surprised I didn't see it right away. I started thinking something was up, but I guess the sight of the beach distracted me."

"I guess it did. The beach is pretty distracting."

"You know, you two were acting kind of weird. Other people are bound to figure it out."

"I am so into him, Kate, no wonder you could pick up on the fact that something was different between us. He's just such an amazing guy—in and out of bed," Lindsey divulged.

"Okay. Gross and weird. He's my brother. I did not need to know that," Kate replied, somewhat kidding.

"But you're my best friend! Pretend I'm talking about someone else then," Lindsey suggested, flopping onto her bed, getting ready for a really good girl talk. Kate followed, sitting cross-legged. Just then, she frowned.

"You guys haven't ... you know, done the deed, in here, have you?" Kate asked, scrunching her nose as she waited for Lindsey's answer.

Lindsey gave her a look in response that said, "Really, Kate?"

Kate shuddered. "I don't know if I can get used to the whole you and my brother together thing. Even though I'd love to have you as my sister!"

Lindsey put up two hands to stop Kate. "Whoa! Whoa, whoa. Let's not get ahead of ourselves here. Especially in regards to anything involving rings or weddings, given my incredibly recent and not-so-pleasant past."

"Yeah, but you and Patrick ... I just couldn't see the two of you happy together for the long run, but I could see you settled with Harris. I've spent a lot of time around you two, though it hasn't been at the same time, but trust me, your personalities just mesh so well."

"Thanks for your expertise, Kate. I really appreciate it," Lindsey said, rolling her eyes.

"Hey, anytime," Kate shrugged.

***

After Kate left to go shower and get dressed for their dinner out, Lindsey straightened her hair and put on a pair of mint shorts and a peach-colored swing top, perfect for dinner out in the Hamptons. It made her heart so happy to be with the whole Welling family. They were such a sweet group of people. She hummed softly as she slipped in a pair of gold earrings and used her macadamia and Argan oil lotion on her arms and legs.

Harris was lingering in the upstairs lounge area by the stairs when she headed out of her room.

"Were you waiting for me?" she asked with her hands on her hips and a broad smile on her face.

"Maybe," he teased. "I wanted to run something by you privately, before we were around everyone else again," he added, taking her hand.

"What's that?" she asked, lacing her fingers between his.

"Now that Kate knows about what's going on between us, are you okay with everyone else knowing about it, too?"

Lindsey mulled it over for a few seconds before she spoke. "Let's still keep our relationship quiet for the time being. Maybe tomorrow or the next day we can tell everyone else, once we've all been around each other a little more. Kate's different. She knows me so well, and she knows I would never treat you like you weren't important or just a careless fling no matter how things eventually ended up between us. Everyone else would just see me as the girl rebounding from a broken engagement, and I don't think that would sit too well with them."

Harris placed his hands on her shoulders and gazed lovingly into her eyes. "No, they wouldn't see it like that. They've all known you for such a long time, and they've known me even longer. I think they'd be happy to know something was happening between us romantically."

"But we're not even sure what's going to happen between us down the road—and you know they'll start asking tons of questions—you won't believe some of the stuff Kate was already coming up with," Lindsey told him, still in awe that Kate had married them off in her mind within two minutes of finding out they were a thing. Her free-spirited friend was a little too far off the reservation with that particular zinger.

"That would be the case no matter what the circumstances." Harris made a good point. Questions would abound when his family found out, whether they'd been in a relationship for months, or if they'd only gone on a single date.

"Let's just give it another day or so, okay? I can't wait for you to secretly sneak in my room later tonight," she bargained seductively.

"How can I deny you that?" he said helplessly in reply.

Chapter 8

"I don't think I could be any happier than I am right now," Lindsey smiled as she laid her head and flung her arm across Harris' bare chest in her darkened bedroom.

He intertwined his fingers through hers. "I feel the same way, Linds."

They lay there in a comfortable, sated silence for several minutes. "I know the circumstances surrounding us getting together weren't all that typical, but I can't help thinking it just feels meant to be, you know?" she dreamily asked right before she drifted off to sleep.

"Absolutely, sweetheart. Absolutely," Harris replied, his lips grazing her forehead, placing a kiss as a gentle as a feather.

Lindsey fell asleep to the steady beating of his heart beneath her ear, more content and carefree than she'd been in as far back as she could remember. She hadn't thought much about Patrick since she'd arrived, especially now, as she was determined not to compare or pick apart Harris based on her previous relationship, but truly, if she were to decide to do so, Harris would blow Patrick out of the water in every way imaginable.

In such a short amount of time, they'd somehow connected on a deep, intangible level that she'd never experienced with another person before. They easily spent time enjoying life together, laughing and teasing, but they also had amazing, serious discussions about life that struck such a chord with her that she dared not imagine what it would be like to go a day without talking to him—about both the big and the little things. Was what they shared just a summer fling? Maybe at first, she could've seen it being something like that, but it certainly didn't feel that way to her anymore.

When she first woke up the next morning, the sheet beside her was sadly cool when she reached for Harris, but as she grew more coherent, the reason for his absence came back to her. She now fully understood his disappointment at her wanting to keep their relationship quiet for a little while longer. It was no fun to know that she would have to start her day without him, and then hope it wasn't all that obvious when she did finally seek him out, unable to stay away any longer.

She didn't have to worry though. As she sat up and stretched, her eyes caught the sticky note stuck on the bedroom mirror. In Sharpie, all it said was "Beach run?" in his thick, slanted writing. She hopped out of bed and hurried to dress in gray workout pants, a violet sports bra and a loose yoga tank. Quickly throwing her hair back, she rushed through the quiet house and out the back door as the sun made its first streaks across the horizon.

She caught sight of his dark hair against the pale sand down on the beach, and made her way down the wooden walkway over the dunes to where he stood, stretching and waiting for her.

"I knew you'd come," he said with a smile.

"I'm always up for a run," she reminded him, dashing off in an attempt to outrun him. He caught up with her within seconds, and they set a leisurely pace together along the shoreline.

***

"Lindsey, someone is at the door for you—they're waiting outside," Harris' brother-in-law Jonathan said with a frown later that night. Her brow furrowed in confusion as she hopped up from her seat between Kate and Harris. She set her hand of cards down on the cocktail table and headed toward the front of the house at a loss as to who would be visiting her. Who could possibly be coming to see her at the Wellings' beach house?

She reached the front door and pulled it open, and when she looked out, her face drained of color. She leaned against the foyer door frame for support, afraid she might faint.

"What are you doing here?" she asked, her breath coming in shallow gasps.

"Lindsey," Patrick said, rushing toward her, his hair dripping wet from the heavy downpour hitting loud against the house. He reached for her hands, but she snatched them back immediately. "I—I had to see you. I realized I made the biggest mistake of my life when I ended our engagement. There's no way I can imagine not marrying you now. I was scared, that's all, and I can't even begin to express how sorry I am," he told her when she offered up no words of warm greeting.

She stared at him, feeling little sympathy, even as his face grew more etched with stress and worry. "What am I supposed to say to that?" she asked stoically.

He dropped to his knees. "Please say you'll forgive me. That you'll take me back and agree to marry me again. Please say those things, Lindsey, or I don't know how I can do life anymore. I love you and these past couple of weeks without you have been completely awful."

"Why didn't you call me?"

"I didn't know what to say that would make you believe how sorry I was over the phone. I knew I'd hurt you, and you deserved a face-to-face apology," he explained.

"Get off the floor, Patrick," she told him impatiently. Glancing behind her, she took a few steps, putting some space between them on the large front porch.

"Let's talk this through for a minute," she said, feeling her resolve soften a bit as she stared down at his desperate face. He jumped up and nodded eagerly. The air beneath the porch's roof was thick and humid as the rain poured around them.

"You hurt me, Patrick. How could I ever trust that you wouldn't go and change your mind about us again?" she demanded, hot tears pricking at her eyes. She realized now more than ever that there was much to be resolved between the two of them.

"Because, Linds. We have five solid years together behind us already. We never had a bump, not even a hiccup in all that time until I stupidly got cold feet at our engagement party. And that had nothing to do with you, babe, it was more about me realizing that I'd gotten to another stage in my life. It freaked me out a little when I realized how quickly life was passing by, but now more than ever I'm sure as hell that I don't want it passing by without you by my side."

Studying the wrecked man before her, thoughts of their late-night pizza runs, romantic movie nights in the park, brunch with his parents, walking on the beach together, the first time they said "I love you," and the day he asked her to marry him all came rushing to her mind, and her heart lurched inside of her chest painfully, torn as it was. Part of her wanted to throw herself into his waiting arms, while the other wanted to run inside and cling to Harris.

"I've spent the last couple of weeks trying to move on, trying to pick up the thousands of pieces of my heart you smashed with those words at your parents' house. And now you're telling me you didn't even mean what you said?" She choked up, but stood her ground. She didn't want him to see her cry.

"I'm telling you that I was an idiot and I can't do anything to change that, but I promise from this very second forward, I will love you forever and I will be by your side through thick and thin. Always." He reached for her again, but she stepped away. This was all too much.

"I need a minute to think, Patrick. My mind is reeling."

"Take all the time you need."

She walked over to the other edge of the porch, and watched the rain pour down in thick sheets. Before Harris was a part of the picture, wasn't this what she had wanted? Her life plan—everything would be back on track if she forgave him. But then there was Harris to consider. She was in love with him, or so she thought. How could she even consider going back to Patrick if she was pretty sure she loved someone else?

But, what she and Harris had could just be a romanticized summer fling, and once they returned to their normal lives, away from the magic of the beach and sunsets, it could very well peter out. Was she really willing to throw away the solid relationship she had with Patrick over a slight possibility that things would work out well with Harris?

She weighed her options carefully, but only grew more confused the more she thought about them. Furiously shaking her head, she crossed the porch once more.

"There's no way that I can tell you at this exact second that we can just pick up where we left off and resume our relationship. There's more at stake than you realize," she sighed. "Are you going back to the city tonight?"

"No, I'm staying at a family friend's house," he told her, looking slightly disappointed with her answer.

"Did you take the jitney?"

"No, I drove."

"If I decide that I think we can actually make this work again, I'll be waiting here on the porch for you at exactly seven in the morning. I'll ride with you back into the city. If I'm not out here, it's over, and I ask that you don't contact me ever again," she said with finality.

"Please, Lindsey, I pray that you'll give us another chance. We have such a strong history and I don't think I'll ever be able to forgive myself for letting one bad choice be the cause of us throwing our relationship away," he said gently, taking both of her hands in his own.

"I told you I would think about it, Patrick. Go now, so I can do just that, please," she replied, pulling her hands away from his.

He nodded vigorously before dashing back out into the rain. She watched as he jumped into his car and pulled out of the drive. She didn't turn away until the red taillights were no longer visible in the dark. Unable to go back inside and join the enthusiastic game night festivities after what had just taken place, she took a seat in one of the rocking chairs lined up across the front porch. She needed to think. What was she going to do?

Neither choice felt like an obvious one. There were a lot of unknowns in regards to Harris. Sure, she felt strongly for him already, but it was all so new ... Then, when it came to Patrick, they'd shared so much, but he'd hurt her so deeply. Could she really forgive him for breaking their engagement the way he did?

Lost in thought, she didn't hear the front door open and close.

"Everything alright, Linds?" Harris asked, taking a seat next to her.

"Hmm?" she asked startled, glancing beside her. "Oh, oh yeah. Everything's fine," she said a little too cheerfully.

"If you don't mind my asking, who was here that wanted to see you?"

"It was just a friend of mine that happens to be staying close by with some of their family for the Fourth. We've been texting and they just stopped by to say hello while they were in the area," she semi-lied.

"Oh, okay. I only ask because it seems like something's wrong. Are you sure you're okay?"

"Yes, I'm sure. Just tired. I think I'm going to head to bed and get some rest. See you in the morning?" she asked, stretching her arms and yawning for emphasis.

"Of course," he said, standing up and reaching his hands out to lift her from her seat. He wrapped his arms around her, holding her close. "I'll miss you, though," he murmured against her hair. She smiled, bittersweet, into his shoulder. When he kissed her goodnight, she kissed him deeply, passionately, not even caring if someone stumbled upon them on the porch. If she decided to leave in the morning, then this would be the last time she ever kissed him, and she was certainly going to make it count.

When she reluctantly left the warmth of his arms, she headed upstairs, her heart weighing heavy in her chest. Guilt laid upon her like a thick, winter blanket. When she reached her room, she shut the door and rested against it with a woeful sigh. No matter what she decided, come tomorrow, someone was going to end up hurt. Betrayed. Angry. And it would be all her fault. No doubt about that.

Even though exhaustion from weighing such a heavy decision seeped into her very bones, sleep did not come for her. She spent the majority of the night tossing and turning, constantly thinking about what she should do, deciding something and then immediately changing her mind. Why was this so hard? Shouldn't she know her own heart?

Even though she had changed her mind at least a dozen times throughout the night, as the first light of dawn crept through the opened blinds, turning her bedroom a sleepy silver gray, she raced out of bed, a decision firmly made. She finally knew what she had to do.

Chapter 9

Lindsey tiptoed as quiet as a mouse into Harris' room. He looked so peaceful, but somehow, also incredibly sexy as he lay there sleeping soundly, his mouth slightly ajar. She watched his bare, muscled chest rise and fall softly as he breathed evenly and her heart lurched. She'd known this wasn't going to be easy, but she'd had no idea how torturous this was truly going to be.

Tearing her eyes away from his cozy, sleeping figure, she dropped the note she'd written for him on the nightstand and snuck silently back out of the room. A lump formed in her throat and tears burned in her eyes. Once again, she found herself questioning her decision. Was choosing Patrick what was really best for her? Shouldn't this be so much easier if leaving with Patrick was the right thing to do?

She shook her head. No, it definitely wasn't easy, but it had to be the right thing. Being with Patrick, picking up where they left off—that was what made the most sense to her. Her life would return back to where it had been—she would be perfectly back on track. The wedding would take place in April, they'd look for a house in Westchester, and they'd eventually settle down and have 2.5 children and a golden retriever. Maybe a goldfish, too. Getting back on track was what she wanted. She strived for order, for plans. Harris had been a wild card. He hadn't been planned. The fling had just happened and left her topsy-turvy. That wasn't her or the way she did things. Now, it was time to get back to reality and her life in the city. Patrick was a part of that.

But why then, was she having the hardest time leaving? As she managed her bulky luggage down the wide staircase, she kept fighting with herself to keep from running and jumping into Harris' bed, snuggling up against him as he slept. She could just march right back up the stairs, grab that letter, tear it up, and no one would ever know that Patrick had even visited the house.

For some reason though, she continued on, one foot marching in front of the other, down the steps, stopping to turn off the alarm code, and then she was out the front door where she would wait for Patrick to arrive.

When his black sedan pulled into the circular drive, she tried her hardest to appear excited. She tried to smile. Putting on a brave front, she firmly believed her happiness and the excitement she'd had for marrying Patrick would soon return. It would just take some time, that was all.

When he pulled to a stop, Patrick jumped out of the car and ran up the steps, scooping her into his arms and kissing her passionately. She wrapped her arms around his neck and squeezed her eyes shut, trying to be in the moment with him.

"I'm so happy to see you here, Lindsey. I promise, sweetie, I will never hurt you like that ever again," he vowed.

She nodded. "I believe you. The past is in the past," she said softly, trying not to cry.

He helped her get her luggage into the trunk and held the door for her when she slipped into the passenger's seat.

"Time to start the rest of our journey together," he said as he pulled away. She nodded absently, unable to remove her eyes from the white clapboard mansion by the sea until it faded from her view.

***

Harris wasn't one to normally sleep late. So rising mid-morning was rare, even more so since sleep still tugged at his eyes. He blamed the beach. Smirking, he thought about how many nights he'd stayed up much later than normal in the past week. Maybe there was more to blame for his unusual tiredness than just the beach. Thinking along those lines, he briefly wondered why Lindsey hadn't snuck into his bed by now. She was probably on a run, or taking a morning swim.

He sat up and stretched. Time to get going. Just as he was about to fling the covers back and hop out of bed, the white paper on the bedside table caught his eye. He saw his name written across the front in a pretty, feminine script. He smiled. Lindsey must have snuck in there and left him a sweet note. He smiled at the gesture—how thoughtful of her.

Picking up the letter, he began to read.

Dear Harris,

First of all, I have to tell you that you mean so much to me. I care about you a lot. A whole lot. Like, way more than I probably should for how short of a time we've been together. That's why I can't bring myself to face you and tell you the truth.

I left this morning for New York. With Patrick. He was the one that stopped by the house last night, and I'm so sorry that I kept the truth about that from you last night. I hated lying to you. He came and begged for my forgiveness and to take him back, and I spent all night trying to figure out what I should do.

After much thought, I've decided to forgive him and try to make things work between us. We have such a history, and I know that he does love me and I did, I mean, I do, love him, too. What's happened between you and me—it's been so amazing. But it's new and exciting and I can't throw away five years on the chance that maybe we'll work out. You know?

I'm so sorry, Harris. I really am. I hope you can forgive me. By the way, no one from your family knows that I've left, but

I'm going to call Kate this afternoon and explain everything, so there's no need for you to mention anything.

Love,

Lindsey

After reading the letter through twice, he stared at the oil painting of a pelican that hung directly across from his bed. He stared so long, he could pick up the subtle changes between the gray and the black, the white of the bird's feathers and the pearlescent shading of the sea sky behind it. Lindsey was gone. She hadn't even been able to face him and say goodbye. To say that he was hurt was an understatement, and maybe she hadn't realized it yet, but he firmly believed that she soon would realize she made the wrong choice.

He jumped out of bed and quickly changed into his running clothes. He couldn't fully process her letter just yet. He needed to run. And think. She'd made a choice. A bad one, but it was still her choice. There was nothing he could do.

***

"What the hell, Lindsey?" Lindsey grimaced as Kate shouted on the other end of the phone later that afternoon.

"I know, I know. I'm sorry. I didn't mean to hurt Harris," Lindsey replied, regret clouding her mind.

"But you did. He won't even talk to me about it. And seriously? I thought you were smart. What on earth made you think it would be a good idea to go back to Patrick? Especially after what he did to you!"

"Kate, I'm sorry if you're upset with me about Harris. I'm upset with myself. But you know that Patrick and I are close. This was a hiccup. We're going to talk about getting the wedding back on track tonight."

"As your best friend, I'm only going to say this one time and then I'll shut my mouth. Don't marry Patrick. I think you're only going back to him because you can fit your life into a tidy plan and this is just a bullet point that will keep you on your idea of a perfect schedule. Regardless of what's going on between you and Harris, I still don't believe Patrick is the right guy for you."

"Wow, Kate. That was ballsy—even for you. I appreciate your concern, I really do, but it isn't necessary. I'm a big girl and I think I know what's best for me. I have a lot of unpacking to do, so I think I better go now. Enjoy the rest of your trip," Lindsey rushed to say, hanging up before Kate could reply. She didn't want to hear any more of Kate's opinions right now. She had to get ready for dinner with Patrick.

An hour later, wearing a dressy black romper and nude, high-heeled sandals, Lindsey left her apartment and met Patrick at Nobu. He looked sharp seated at the bar in a sleek pair of pants and a button-down shirt. She eased onto the barstool beside him. He nudged a cucumber martini, her favorite drink at Nobu, toward her.

"Thank you," she said sweetly before taking a sip of the tangy drink.

"You're welcome. I know they're your favorite. Our table should be ready shortly," he told her. He was right. Before she'd even finished her drink, the hostess came over and let them know that their table was ready.

Once they were seated and they'd ordered, Patrick sat back and folded his hands on the table. "Okay, Lindsey. I have something big that I need to discuss with you."

She arched an eyebrow at him, his ominous voice freaking her out a little. "Sure, you can talk to me about anything." *Despite the fact that I'm holding back on telling you that I had a fling with someone else for the brief week and a half that we were apart,* she mentally added.

"I think we should move up the date of our wedding."

Lindsey almost spit out her drink at his unexpected words. "Wait, what?"

He repeated his statement and added, "Look, I know that I want to be married to you. End of story. But all the planning and details and craziness ... that's what freaks me out. I just wanted to throw the idea out for a simpler, more casual wedding ... possibly this fall."

"This fall?" She asked incredulously. That was so soon!

He nodded. "Yeah, maybe fifty people or so on my parents' estate. Something small and intimate."

Patrick wanted to move the wedding up a considerable amount of time. She was still having a hard time wrapping her head around that fact, despite his reiterating his words and even providing an actual way to implement his changes. "It takes a lot to plan a wedding," she said slowly, hoping to point out the obvious.

"Between you and my mother, I know it can be done. You guys are like the celebrities of party planning. Besides, if you agree to a smaller wedding, it will be even easier to handle the details quickly."

She played with the straw in her drink, staring intensely at the glass. What was she supposed to say? Isn't this what she wanted? What she'd hoped and planned for since she and Patrick had hit the three-year mark so long ago?

"Okay, yes. Sure. Let's do it," she said, looking up and not thinking anymore.

His face lit up and he looked almost relieved. "Great! Why don't we start looking at dates?" he asked, pulling out his phone. Lindsey put up a hand to stop him.

"This was such a huge game changer. I'll look at my calendar when I get home and we can decide on a date tomorrow. Right now, let's talk about something else," she told him.

He stuck his phone back in his pocket. "Okay, that's fine. What do you want to talk about?"

She racked her brain, sort of wishing they had just been talking about dates after all since the only conversation topic popping into her head was confessing her fling with Harris. She shoved the bright, vivid memories down and shook her head to rid herself of their lingering effects.

"Um, did you tell your parents about our breakup?" she asked.

He looked sheepish. "No, I didn't, but I'm glad. It makes things much less awkward. Did you tell Joe and Tammy?"

She shook her head. "I couldn't bring myself to do it, so my parents are none the wiser either. They're all still going to be super surprised when they hear that we've decided to move the wedding up six months."

"Yeah, that's true. They'll probably think you're pregnant."

She laughed. "It's not the eighteenth century. If I was pregnant, no one would care enough to be outraged."

"That's true. So, you'll tell your parents and I'll tell mine?"

"Sounds like a plan."

They talked and laughed as they ate and for a brief second, it felt to Lindsey like the past two weeks had never happened—that they hadn't broken up, and she hadn't met and fallen for someone else, spending days and nights in his arms happy and content. But the moment was fleeting and she remembered once again that her heart wasn't just her fiancé's anymore, no matter how much she wished it otherwise.

Chapter 10

July turned to August which swept into September before Lindsey realized it. Caught up in wedding planning, she hardly had time to think, much less feel. The day had arrived for her first wedding shower and she rose feeling a little less than eager for the event to take place. It might have had something to do with her mother adding Kate's mother to the guest list. Sure, Gina Welling didn't know that she'd had a fling with her son, but it didn't make it any less awkward. Besides, she and Kate were barely on toleration terms thanks to what had happened at the beach. Lindsey didn't blame Kate for being pissed. She would have been, too, had the tables been turned. Thank God, she had forgiven her, at least, and agreed to be her maid of honor once more.

At two o'clock on the dot, Kate and Mrs. Welling were the last guests to walk through the door of Lindsey's parents' Long Island home. They couldn't have looked more opposite with Kate wearing a vibrant blue jumpsuit, heels and a headband and Mrs. Welling in a navy, age-appropriate pantsuit, her hair suitably styled in a classic cut. But the comradeship and affection between them was palpable.

Lindsey adjusted her cinched emerald dress that grazed just above her knee and greeted the duo, even as her stomach knotted uncomfortably. Gina, as she insisted everyone call her, gave Lindsey a warm hug and commented on her lovely dress. Kate gaze wasn't all that friendly, but she kept quiet. Lindsey prayed no one noticed the strain between them.

After the cake had been cut, Lindsey sought out Kate. She found her sipping sangria out on the patio with a couple of their friends. "Kate, can I talk to you for a minute?"

Kate nodded and hopped up from her seat. "Sure, anything for the bride," she replied coolly.

Kate followed her to her childhood bedroom. Lindsey shut the door behind them to give them a little bit of privacy. "We have to put an end to this," Lindsey started.

"An end to what?" Kate asked, confused.

"The weirdness between us."

"You slept with my brother and got back with your fiancé whom you happened to not tell about my beloved brother. Sorry if I'm not necessarily thrilled with this marriage of yours. I'm by your side, aren't I?"

"I said I was sorry. What am I supposed to do? Tell Patrick I slept with someone within a week after we broke up? That I had serious feelings for someone else and still think about that person all the time?" Lindsey cried.

"I knew you still had feelings for him!" Kate said, pointing her finger.

"What does it matter? I made a choice! I'm not going back on it now," Lindsey replied.

"It matters a lot. I think Harris still has feelings for you, too. He moved to the city last month, you know. He lives less than two blocks from you."

"I didn't know that. Why didn't you tell me?"

"You made me swear not to talk about Harris with you. Remember?"

"Yeah, well you shouldn't have listened to me."

Kate rolled her eyes. "He keeps to himself. He's a writer. He won't bother you or rat you out to that loser—I mean, Patrick."

"I'm not worried about that. It just would've been nice to know."

"Lindsey, please, think about what you're doing. I know I've already said it once and promised not to question you again, but if you still have feelings for Harris, that has to mean something."

"It means I got caught up in the fantasy of something. The time at the beach we shared together wasn't real life."

"Okay, tell yourself whatever helps you sleep at night, Linds. I love you, girl, and I'll be by your side no matter who you marry because I'm your best friend, but please think long and hard about it, okay?" Kate pulled her into a big bear hug before leaving her to go back to the party.

Lindsey plopped down onto the polka-dotted aqua comforter. She should go back to the shower—it was for her, after all. But she didn't want to move. All of these traditional wedding moments—dress shopping, cake tasting, showers in her honor—she'd looked forward to them all since she was a little girl, but now that they were here, she dreaded each and every event.

Taking a deep breath, she left her childhood retreat and joined the other women mingling in the home's common areas. Her grandmother wished her lifetime of happiness, and Aunt Bev handed her a book of healthy recipes she'd printed "off the line," as she referred to the internet. As the house full of women ate finger sandwiches and tea cakes, she opened dozens of wonderful presents and she smiled so much her cheeks ached. But the ache didn't hold a candle to the one deep within her heart.

Chapter 11

October 10th

Wedding Day

Not a hair was out of place. Her stylist, Enrique, had given her reddish-brown tresses the royal treatment and the intricate updo with braids and curls was worthy of a princess, or at least, a duchess. Her dress, a custom creation by Pallas, a dear friend of Kate's from design school, fit her like a glove and managed to balance a classic, retro beauty with modern lines and beadwork. Everything looked perfect—exactly like she'd always wanted.

"Oh, Lindsey," her mother gushed, tearing up when she first saw her daughter ready to walk down the aisle in the Crawfords' large guest bedroom that had been turned into a bridal suite.

"Mom," she whispered, squeezing her mother's hand. All too soon, it was time for Mrs. Thomas to be ushered down the aisle. She watched as her mother made her way down the linen runner perfectly placed across the Crawfords' palatial lawn between the rows of wooden chairs. Swaths of ivory, cream and peach roses and lanterns lined both sides of the aisle. All of their family and friends were there. Kate made her way down the aisle in a vintage navy Valentino gown, and from where she waited in the sunroom, Lindsey saw Patrick, all smiles waiting at the end of the aisle in front of the arbor of roses and vines strung with lights. It was quite possibly the most romantic setting she'd ever seen in person.

"Ready, pumpkin?" her father asked, offering her his arm.

She nodded. "As ready as I'll ever be," she replied, much too halfheartedly for what was supposed to be the happiest day of her life.

The string quartet began to play an instrumental version of John Legend's "All of Me" and she stepped down the aisle to her future. As the music swirled in the twilight, the cool, late afternoon breeze picked up and she shivered. She glanced at Patrick, and smiled. This was what she wanted. This was the plan. They were going to be happy.

She reached the arbor and took Patrick's hand in hers. He looked at her lovingly, and she shared a smile with him. This was it. The moment they'd waited for was finally here.

"Dearly beloved, we are gathered here today ..." the minister began and she tuned out a bit. Not on purpose, it was simply a little overwhelming standing in front of 75 people who were watching her promise to love someone and stick by him for the rest of her life.

"If anyone has any objections to the union of Patrick and Lindsey, speak now or forever hold your peace," she heard the minister say, vaguely wondering why she hadn't asked for him to take out that antiquated line.

"I do!"

Lindsey's eyes grew wide as she heard Harris' voice behind her. She slowly turned to see him standing from his seat with his family. She hadn't even realized he was there until this very moment. He hurried through the seats and into the aisle, running to Lindsey.

"I thought I could sit there and let you do this, but I can't, Lindsey. I love you and I need you to know that. If you were worried that what we had was just a fling, I'm sorry, it wasn't. Not for me, at least. I want to be with you—wake up with you every day, fall asleep with you each night. Please, don't marry someone else," he said before Patrick interrupted him.

"Who the hell do you think you are?" he asked sharply.

Lindsey placed a hand on his arm. "Patrick, wait, please."

"What is he talking about, Lindsey?" he asked quietly.

"He … I …" Lindsey, stammered, not sure how to answer her groom. She glanced over at Harris, and suddenly, everything came into perfect focus. "I'll have to explain later. Right now, you need to know that, I'm sorry, but there's no way I can marry you," she replied, handing the bridal bouquet of peach peonies, cream roses and baby's breath to a waiting, supremely happy, Kate. She even gave her a little thumbs-up.

She had eyes only for Harris, seeing nothing around her—not the wedding party, or the confused faces of their guests, or the beautiful décor surrounding them on the lawn—only Harris, and everything within her was at peace. She took the hand he held outstretched to her, and they ran down the aisle toward the parked cars as everyone looked on in shock. She was pretty sure she even heard Mrs. Crawford gasp.

"What do we do now?" Lindsey asked as they ran from the ceremony site. She held her gown's bustles of silk and tulle off of the ground, but the heeled sandals she wore didn't allow her to do much more than slowly jog alongside Harris. However, her adrenaline was in high gear. What if Patrick decided to run after them?

"We get out of here," he said, reaching in his pocket and pulling out his car keys as they ran. "You know, I'm so glad Kate talked me into coming, but just for the record, I hadn't planned on standing up in the middle of your wedding. I parked on the edge over here." He hit the unlock button and the lights of a red Jeep briefly flashed as they reached it. He opened the door and helped her into the passenger's seat, stuffing the train of her dress inside the small vehicle. Once she was settled in, he ran around and jumped into the driver's seat, turning the ignition and peeling off before speaking another word.

They rode away, volumes of billowy white fabric filling his Jeep's small interior. Lindsey breathed deeply, trying not to feel suffocated by the dress that only moments earlier she'd believed to be the most beautiful gown in the entire world.

"So what do we do now?" Lindsey repeated.

Harris took her hand in his, intertwining his fingers between hers and softly kissing the inside of her wrist. "Truthfully, I don't care what we do, as long as I'm with you, I'm happy."

"I didn't say it out there, but I love you, Harris. There wasn't a day that went by that I didn't think about you, and go back and forth about whether I made a mistake or not leaving that morning."

"I love you, too, Lindsey. I wish I would have sought you out sooner, but I was determined to give you your space, be happy for you. I came today as a sort of closure, wanting to truly be happy for you, but as you walked down the aisle, all I could see was a strange, bittersweet sadness in your eyes. It definitely didn't seem like the way a happy bride should look. I knew right then that I had to save you from yourself."

"I'm so glad you did! I hate that I hurt Patrick, but how could I have been so stupid?" she asked, confused about what had possessed her to go through the motions like that. It had been so wrong of her.

"You were trying to live up to your own expectations and timelines. What we had, in such a short amount of time, didn't make sense to you. I get that—I really do, but I love you and I'm here—not going anywhere. Ever."

She smiled at him. "You should write a romance novel. You're really good at figuring out the flawed female character obviously."

"You're not flawed, and I think I'll stick to thrillers."

"Harris, everyone is flawed in some sort of way. I'm sorry that my flaws hurt you, and ended up hurting someone else, too," she added sadly.

"I love that you care so much about others, Lindsey, but if I had to say there was a particular flaw about you, it would be that you care too much about how others are going to feel, even when making them comfortable or doing what they want is detrimental to you."

"Pretty sure most people would say that I'm anal about plans and schedules—that's my flaw," she remarked.

"Well, yeah, there's that, too, but I personally love that about you—seeing as I'm a bit of a punctual stickler myself."

Her mouth dropped open. "How in the world did you ever survive living in the same house with Kate?"

He laughed. "I managed. But I don't want to talk about Kate right now. I literally just left a wedding that wasn't my own with the bride."

"You sure did."

Harris drove, but to Lindsey's surprise, instead of heading into the city, he veered off onto the Long Island Expressway. She stared at him in confusion.

"I thought it would be a good idea to go back to where it all began—the beach house," he said, kissing the top of her hand, and her insides turned to mush.

"Perfect," she replied, starry-eyed and full of hope for their beautiful future.

Epilogue

Their wedding wasn't planned. Well, in Lindsey's view of things, it wasn't planned. Two weeks before the annual Welling beach trip the following year, Harris proposed. As he rose from one knee from the candlelit rooftop of his building, sliding the three-carat, emerald-cut ring onto her finger, Lindsey had an idea.

"What if we get married at the beach?" she asked spontaneously.

"I'm sure we can get married at the beach," Harris answered.

"I know, but I mean, we're going there anyway for the Fourth, my family lives less than an hour from there … what do you think?"

"Sure," Harris replied without a moment's hesitation.

And he held her to her original idea, even when her neurotic need for details and schedules didn't coincide with her random, romantic spontaneity and affinity for their moments at the beach.

But with the help of Kate, Gina and her mother, they'd thrown together an intimate gathering at dusk, complete with a silk-paneled tent and oceanside reception.

She didn't walk down the aisle to Harris, they walked down the aisle together. They repeated vows they'd written to one another, and of course, Harris' were so perfectly written they made her cry. She felt like a teenager with her first note to a crush in comparison, but he seemed to like what she said.

After their kiss, the pronouncement and a party that lasted well into the night, Harris carried her upstairs,

"Are you happy, Mrs. Welling?"

She laughed, so happy she couldn't contain it with just a smile. "I think I might just be the happiest bride that ever existed," she said, completely believing her every word.

What to read next?

If you liked this book, you will also like *Dangerous Treasure*. Another interesting book is *Taming the Billionaire*.

Dangerous Treasure

Jana Sebastian is never at home. Her work as an archaeologist keeps her living out of suitcases and tents in remote locations all across the globe. On her latest dig in California, she meets charismatic Pete Abernathy, a former combat engineer who now specializes in setting up structured camps for archaeology expeditions. What begins as playful banter soon grows into something much more personal as they seek a lost golden treasure. However, a missing artifact changes everything as their newly formed bond is put to the ultimate test of trust. With both their reputations at stake, will they be able to salvage their careers without casting suspicion on one another? Follow them on a harrowing journey as a mysterious theft leads them not only to the brink of despair, but ultimately takes them on a whirlwind ride where they learn more about the true character of one another than they could have ever imagined.

Taming the Billionaire

Kate Hensley sells her handmade soap on the internet and works in her best friend's bar to make ends meet. When a new resort comes to her hometown, she takes a chance and schedules a meeting with the CEO to get her soaps in the resort. What she doesn't plan on is the CEO, Luke Wilder, being so handsome and very arrogant. A chance encounter resulting in a fender bender gets them off on the wrong foot and she thinks that she'll never get her foot in the door. But when they happen to meet again, they end up apologizing to each other and to Kate's surprise Luke asks her out on a date. Suddenly Kate's life goes from strictly business to whirlwind dates with the handsome CEO. She enjoys his company and it isn't long before her heart is lost to him. Just when she thinks everything is going right in her life, she finds out something that may destroy it all.

About Olivia West

Olivia West is a bestselling romance author who is known for her captivating stories with interesting characters, unusual settings, adventurous plots and intriguing relationships. In each of her stories she tries to make readers see in their imagination a mental movie in which they can feel emotions of the characters and are curious about what will happen next.

One Last Thing…

If you believe that *The Stolen Bride* is worth sharing, would you spend a minute to let your friends know about it?

If this book lets them have a great time, they will be enormously grateful to you – as will I.

Olivia

www.OliviaWestBooks.com

Made in the USA
Monee, IL
11 July 2020